Green Roses

Petals and Thorns

Tatenda Charles Munyuki

By The Same Author

XCLUSIVE ZONE ANGELS: The Chosen Ones
XCLUSIVE ZONE ANGELS: The Adamant Genesis
XCLUSIVE ZONE ANGELS: The Odd Temptations
XCLUSIVE ZONE ANGELS: The Sacred Secrets
LOTANDO UREY: The Torture Chamber
LOTANDO UREY: Servitude Defined
GREEN ROSES: Petals and Thorns
The Circumcision of Adam and Eve
The Naked Teenager
The Angry Girlchild
The Cruel Kiss
Inhumanity

NACH (The Adventures of Nathan Amanda Chenai Hama) Series
THE MONTE CHICKS Series
BATTLE OF SEXES Series
PU$HERZ Series

AGENTS Series

Green Roses

Petals and Thorns

Tatenda Charles Munyuki

Darling Kind Publishing

GREEN ROSES: Petals and Thorns

First published in Zimbabwe in 2014
Darling Kind Publishing
an imprint of Tatenda Charles Munyuki Publishing

Copyright © Tatenda Charles Munyuki 2014
Cover Illustration Copyright© Straightline Designz 2014
Cover illustration by Straightline Designz 2014

ISBN   978 0 7974 6164 2

Printed and bound by Darling Kind Publishing, Harare, Zimbabwe.
darlingkindp@live.com

facebook.com/tatendacmunyuki

www.tcmpublishingzim.com

To all my friends...

The Thorns

BEAUTY TO them was a matter of perception. *Was it that this young lady was extremely attractive in a way that was fairly unusual and special, or did she have an attractive face and was also good looking, but not in an unusual way?* Whatever she was, they had agreed on one thing though. She was sitting with the wrong dude.

The two boys sat at one of the recreational park benches, killing the lunchtime. The park was a set of unpreserved vegetation and a couple of ageing buildings. Once a stunning environment, it had transformed into a rigid landscape that people had only compulsorily gotten used to. However, its current state didn't prevent a few individuals and lovebirds to linger and enjoy its only remaining pride. The park was a pretty quiet and peaceful surrounding that minded its own business.

Anesu and Shingi sat a few or so meters from the two *lovebirds* and observed as the male bird skilfully courted the female bird. As it appeared, the female bird had possibly arrived at the park unaccompanied, either from the library or wherever. The male bird must have been alone in the park at that moment. His books lay open on another bench not far from the young lady's spot, and the wind was having fun flipping their pages so vibrantly they looked as if they were going to be ripped off at any moment. Swept off their senses after a rather long span in the library, Anesu and Shingi took interest in the first thing they saw and, for now, it was the boy and girl who sat at a site not so far from the bench they were sitting.

'Mr Dongo, Mr Dongo,' Shingi began with both his hands supporting his head by the chin as he sat with his back arched forward. 'Mr Dongo, you come here to study, yet I don't see any compasses, T-squares, set squares – what have you. I wonder, only wonder.'

Anesu grinned. 'What's on your mind, Shingi? Don't act like you don't know that, for almost everything, there is a theoretical side just as there is a practical one. The library provides me with the former.'

'I know, Mr Dongo, no need to get all academic with me. What I meant was, every time I look up from my own books, all I see in front of you is that *old book*.'

'I like studying how people think, it's fascinating,' Anesu explained in a determined tone. 'Anyway, I'm on holiday, I don't have anything to read like you, Mr Vet.'

Shingi shrugged and frowned as he witnessed the female bird smile at a joke the male bird had cracked. She ended up laughing and as angelic as her laugh was, Shingi felt uncomfortable.

'Can you tell me something about that girl, Mr Dongo, what would your old book say about her?'

'Hours of continuous reading can make one horny.'

'Yeah, right,' Shingi muttered.

'Okay, I can tell you what I can see and well…' Anesu hesitated, biting his lower lip and evaluating the lady, '… what I can do for you if you are serious.'

Shingi stared at him expectantly. 'Let's hear it.'

'Firstly, one has to ask what in the world is she doing out here, I never saw her in the library. That *chimoko's* physical attractiveness can be wrongly viewed and give her attributes such as, she is less modest, is sexually warmer and more socially skilled, more extravert, friendly and mentally healthier. It could be true, but then it could all be false. So, since I don't know her, I can't tell you anything about her that you don't see already, Shingi,' Anesu approved what he had said by nodding.

'What about the part *"…what I can do for you"*' Shingi said.

Anesu's eyes were filled with a spark of life Shingi only saw when his friend was about to suggest or do something unexpected.

'Are you serious, do you want to have a small chat with her?' he asked mysteriously.

Shingi eyed him curiously. 'Hell yeah, but I can't just go over there and say, *"Hi, Mr, can you give me some time alone with this lady you are hitting on?"* can I?'

'Ok, Shingi, but remember that after this you will owe me big time.'

Before Shingi could even reply, Anesu stood up and walked towards where the two lovebirds were perched.

Is he nuts? Shingi thought horrified. He wanted to close his eyes, but had to keep them open when he saw Anesu divert from the path to end up at the bench that held the dude's books.

Anesu picked up what looked like a textbook, and like a madman suddenly hit by a blitz of insanity, took off running in the other direction from that partition of the park. The dude, lady and Shingi stared after him, bewildered. The dude suddenly realized that he was being robbed and he took off after Anesu – hot in pursuit.

A minute passed before Shingi contemplated the whole idea behind Anesu's insane risky act. Afraid of letting his friend down, he cleared his throat, shrugged his weary shoulders and got up. *The ewe had been left unattended.*

The *kombi's* conductor slid the door open for Sue and waited until she had cleanly gotten off. It amused him just how elegant this girl looked in uniform.

'Convent is cooler than I thought, wow!' she said to herself as she walked along the unpaved dusty path that had been eroded by being used as a shortcut to where her neighbourhood was located.

Aggressive shouts made her look up. A guy ran towards her grasping an old battered textbook. Another dude was cursing him, struggling to catch up. As the one being chased passed her, their eyes met and held. Sue saw something in Anesu's eyes that kept her vision fixed at him from a couple of meters away. Although he was running away, Anesu's eyes didn't leave hers for that brief moment. He must have run for fifty meters from where Sue was when he suddenly stopped and stooped over to catch his breath.

When his pursuer passed Sue, she saw so much rage on his face she felt a shiver creep up her spine. The dude looked as if he could momentarily murder someone without preamble. Sue wondered why the one being chased had stopped. She stopped walking and looked back to witness what was going to happen. If there was going to be a fight, she knew that the boy who was being chased wouldn't have the slightest of chances or hope. He would be devastated.

The pursuer reached Anesu and swung a furious right hook that was meant knock the life out of him. Anesu fortunately ducked just in time and locked his arms around the dude. The dude fought barbarically to be released, but Anesu made sure there wasn't even an inch of space between them.

Glued to her spot, Sue watched fixated as the two struggled with each other. It did look ridiculously funny. What amused her most was the fact that Anesu had the chaser in a tight bear-hug lock. He was apparently laughing, saying something at the same time as if it was some sort of a game. Minutes passed and the aggressive chaser stopped struggling and Anesu released him immediately and offered him the book explaining something she couldn't hear. Afraid that the chaser would strike Anesu the moment he was given the chance, Sue couldn't help sighing in relief when Anesu offered a hand and the dude shook it after slight hesitation shrugs.

Now at peace, the two returned along the path, Anesu doing most of the talking. The chaser was apparently trying hard to stay angry, but the grin he wore widened with each step and each word Anesu spoke to him. They passed her once more. The owner of the book stared at her for a few seconds. Antithesis, Anesu didn't even show any sign of acknowledging her existence. To Sue, that felt odd for she was often used to turning heads any time, at any place, in any attire.

'I'm sorry, man, but you see we live in a world full of insane people. I was just unfortunate to be born one of them. How about I buy you some airtime to make up for the trouble?' She heard Anesu saying, producing a dollar from his pocket.

His voice had that sort of mysteriousness in it that had Sue confused for a while. Mesmerized, she found herself blushing when Anesu unexpectedly turned, looked back at her and gave her a simple smile. For someone who had never been so moved by a simple smile to the extent of feeling her heart race uncontrollably, she gasped for air and fought with confusion.

The Petals

REBECCA'S SEMESTER holiday privileged her with having morning shifts at the industry. That provided her with the ability to return home after one o'clock in the afternoon, prepare food for her Grandpa, read a little and mostly enjoy sleep at night.

That afternoon, she had met one of her friends from school and had endured her friend's complains about power cuts in her area. Rebecca felt for her friend. Power cuts were something she rarely suffered in her uneven life. Her grandparents' small house was situated on the outskirts of Mbare, overlooking the main road of Simon Mazorodze. As such, a few houses had their power lines routed together with those of the industries in Southerton and these never experienced power cuts. Rebecca's house was one of those.

It was currently a few minutes after seven evening time and she walked briskly along her street subconsciously admiring the neon lights produced by cars whizzing up and down the main road. Rebecca's mind was saturated by fresh images of her neighbour's cute chubby baby. She was glad that she had finally paid the mother a visit for the lady was one of those lovely neighbourhood women who had helped her and Grandpa get through the thick and thin after Grandma died. She wished Grandpa could have seen the baby, it was so sweet, but Grandpa could barely walk that far nowadays.

"I save my energy for the much desired bathroom fun, my dear."

Rebecca laughed as she remembered her Grandpa's favourite speech whenever she tried to get him outside the gate, more or less the house itself.

Her attention was brought back to the present when one of the hood's tramps suddenly appeared out of nowhere from the dark. The tramp had in his grasp a bottle of beer that looked cleaner than any part of his anatomy. A filthy rucksack was thrown over his left shoulder and his rotten teeth even seemed visible from the dark. He was inebriated, that was for sure. A variety of tones effused from the tramp's throat as he tried to sing and walk properly at the same time.

Life for many people differed and so many were rich as so many poorer. The imbalance was so severe to overlook. Less people were trying so hard to do something about it, but it wasn't good enough than if half of the world tried with them.

Rebecca was too distracted by thoughts of how unfortunate his life was to warn him that small street or not, the tarred road was made for the automobiles first, pedestrians after.

The collision brought such a shattering noise that made her jump violently. The sound of tires producing friction with the road was associated with the smell of burnt rubber.

Instinct made Rebecca sprint towards the knocked over tramp. The headlights of a silver Mercedes shone over them like an operating theatre. The tramp lay on the tar like someone in a coma, his bottle having landed and shattered into pieces at a distance.

'Is he still alive?'

The voice came over her head and, stunned, Rebecca looked up shielding her eyes from the headlight's blinding light. Despite the odd circumstance, her heart missed a few beats as she glared at the owner of the car. She could see both fear and hope in his eyes.

'Is he still alive?' he repeated confused, staring down relentlessly at the tramp he had hit.

Rebecca placed her palm at the tramp's heart rather than the usual pulse checking position – something her system had gotten accustomed to – and baffled the man standing over her considering the state of the tramp.

'He is alive, but he needs to be checked for possible multiple contusions or internal bleeding by a specialist – immediately,' Rebecca shouted back at him, and suddenly felt the tramp's heart slowly begin to fail.

Likewise, she panicked. Then the heart *stopped*.

'Oh, God!' she screamed, ripping off the tramp's dirt moulded jacket and rucksack.

'What, what is it?' the man panicked holding his head. 'What is it, what are you doing?' he produced an iPhone and tried to dial emergency numbers, but the phone slipped, fell to the tar and cracked making him jump and shake even more with fear. He stared down at the tramp in horror and trembled.

Rebecca knelt beside the tramp. There was only one thing to do when the pulse failed. The tramp was slowly leaving this world in which he had lived like vermin. She produced her phone and used its torch facility to check his pupils quickly, ignoring the questions and shouts from the driver who was now pacing to and from above her looking for help. Unfortunately, there was nobody in the street except the three of them. One thing was hopeful though. The tramp's pupils were still equal and active, Rebecca analysed with some difficulty.

She could still somehow save the tramp from the tentacles of death. Automatically, Rebecca adjusted the tramp's head, tilted it back to clear his stench-emitting throat and folded her hands together over his sternum. Her weight concentrated on her arms, she began to apply CPR.

Fifteen firm heels of her hands to his sternum, then two deep exhalations into his mouth pinching his nose as she did so. The tramp's mouth was indeed rile and carious, and she almost swayed into an uncompromising nausea. The owner of the car looked down at them, barely breathing. Dizziness welled up on him like a tide of darkness.

CPR was so demanding that no one person could sustain it alone for more than a few minutes.

'Please, breathe, please!' Rebecca muttered along the fifteen depressions and the two mouthfuls.

The air seemed to defy her lungs. She put her ear just above the tramp's mouth with expectation. Cursing loudly, she resumed her CPR. Failure and exhaustion made her heart tremble, and tears of ire and need ran hotly down her cheeks.

Her face was suddenly splattered with vomit as the tramp resuscitated. It smelt disgusting like a mixture of rotten eggs and decayed vegetables. Clumsily and hastily wiping off her face, Rebecca watched the tramp consume throaty gulps of air. Blurred and musky about what had happened, he tried to sit, but failed dismally.

Rebecca stood up with an effort and felt dizzy for a while. Her knees ached and she could hardly stand straight without falling over. She then felt her body being supported gently, and unwillingly, she slumped against it – unable to resist the aid. The owner of the car planted an affectionate kiss on her delicate forehead and wiped off her tears. Rebecca looked up and saw that he too was now crying.

'Thank you, good Lord, thank you, lady,' his voice was choked with emotion and tenderness.

Rebecca, who had never been in another man's arms before, suddenly remembered where she was and – fighting an odd reluctance – softly pushed away from him. 'He still needs help.' She scanned the tramp who now had his back rested against the Mercedes's bumper, devouring all the night's air he could get without suffocating.

'Please, leave that to me, I'll take him to the hospital right away,' the owner of the car regained enough self-command to be active. 'Can you please help me lift him into the back seat?'

Together, they meticulously carried the tramp and laid him along the backseat with a little difficulty.

'Can we go together, to the hospital I mean?' the man asked, already opening the passenger's door for her.

'I'd have liked to, but someone at home is waiting for me.'

'Oh, you are married,' there was a slight twinge of disappointment in the man's voice.

Flustered and all, the lady in front of him looked like a cherub from a dream. Her eyes looked as if they were constantly smiling at him in a teasing way, whilst also seeming curious at the same moment. Somehow, it made him think of someone, but couldn't really place it. He had to force himself to stop staring at her.

'I'm truly sorry. I've got supper to prepare. Since I left in the afternoon and since he doesn't know how to cook for himself anymore, he must be starving right now,' Rebecca emphasized, looking back directly at the man observing his apparent shyness and mostly his boyish like cuteness. She quickly looked away, to the tramp. 'Don't worry, he won't die. Just make sure you get him to a hospital as soon as you can. I wonder if they'll take him in – he can barely afford to buy himself food, what more a hospital bed? I wish I had some money so that I could give it to you to make sure that he gets some medical attention. Shame,' Rebecca added sadly, gazing at the tramp through the backseat's window. He looked peaceful enough, sleeping in that nice car.

'I'm responsible for this mess whether he was right or wrong. I'll be entitled to see that he gets and receives the best medical help. Please don't worry yourself about anything.' The man put his hand on her fragile arm. He was so touched that someone could be so kind and caring – even for an old filthy stray tramp. Tears began to re-trickle from his sore eyes.

'Would you really do that?' Rebecca jerked her head up, surprised. 'Oh, thank you!' She made a move to hug him, but abruptly stopped herself, inwardly cursing her emotions of trying to get the better of her.

The silver Mercedes raced off and left Rebecca staring after it enchanted. The crickets cricked in the lonely night and so suddenly did she realize that nobody had witnessed the accident and its outcome. Only then was she aware of what she had done to save the tramp, and the owner of the car and the stench of the vomit on her. The driver's visage floated in her mind with all states of its anxiety and relief, but that didn't even tint how handsome he had looked.

Rebecca didn't have time for the opposite sex, or had ever been attracted to any. She lacked interest and her life wasn't one on which she could afford such luxuries, or necessities as some would claim. But something had been ignited in her, and all she could do was to blame it all on the adrenaline rush she had experienced applying CPR and, yet she couldn't help feeling a bit sad that she hadn't obtained the man's name and that he had gone without knowing hers.

Maybe they would meet again someday, she thought. Or, maybe, it was one of those things that came first time and that first time had another definition called *"the last time."*

Rebecca turned around and started for home. Her foot suddenly stepped on something soft and, for a moment, she feared she had stepped on a rodent or something eerie. She looked down and curiously picked it up. It was a black leather wallet and she knew whom it belonged to.

One

DUSK WAS falling as Steve drove back to Mount Pleasant. The first street lights came on as his car negotiated the corner from Norfolk Road, and his father's mansion loomed ahead of him.

There was obviously nothing to be done, he thought defeated. *SteelWorks (Pvt) Ltd.'s* representatives were just being difficult.

The electronic gate patiently opened for him and a few minutes later, he was met at the door by their senior house aid, Ms Sandati. Ms Sandati was a beautiful light-skinned, curvy, middle height woman with an amazing jet of black hair that seemed to style itself without the assistance of a hair salon or chemicals. She had been with the family for about twenty-five years now – since she started working for them as a young adult. Ms Sandati didn't look her age and occupation for she was too attractive and sweet, but Steve guessed her to be in her mid-forties.

Steven Pye was the sole known heir of a multi-millionaire, Richard Lewis Pye the owner of *Pye Industries*. Pye Industries was the legacy of the Pye genealogy since its establishment in 1960. The family company had grown from a small entity into a huge organization to date. Sons and daughters had carried the torch one after the other for the last half-century and had produced the enormous wealth the Pyes now enjoyed in their daily lives.

Richard had taken over the Pye business after his father had died from a scandal that had stirred the family for a decade. Richard had only been twenty-three years old at the time, and many of his uncles had tried endlessly to upset the traditional inheritance structure. However, Richard's mother was one fierce lady and she had fought to the brim with her deceased husband's brothers to prevent such an upheaval. Rumour had it that after a failed attempt on her life and Richard's by one of the uncles, she had retaliated and the uncle who had devised the coup had suddenly disappeared never to be heard of or found again. Nobody had messed with mother and son from then.

Richard had grown into a world of leading a company he had no knowledge or interest in, but he had learned to love the company with age. Richard had met Agnes Marlow shortly after he had turned twenty-six. They had wed within a month of courtship and the result was little Steven Richard (jnr) Pye. The happiness had lasted for four years before Agnes eloped with a former high school lover, with whom she had met two years after Steve's birth and had an affair with till the day she had mastered enough courage to run away with him. Agnes was found a month later, her body bearing marks of extreme violence and struggle, deposited in a ditch. Agnes's lover was found dead that very same week, in the same ditch on the same spot. Richard had been thoroughly investigated as a suspect then, but nothing sinister was discovered on him.

Richard had kept Ms Sandati to raise his only son and heir to the Pye Empire. The questions of why a black woman would solely facilitate the growth of a white child were a controversial issue throughout the society those days, but Richard had cared less. Agnes's betrayal had affected him too much to care about anything else, but his son.

'Hi, Ma,' Steve gave Ms Sandati a peck on the cheek. 'Is Father around?'

Used to being called *Ma* by the Steve since he was seven years old, Ms Sandati embraced him softly. 'He left for SA early in the morning just after you left. He said he needed to have his monthly check up a little bit early this time.'

Steve frowned. 'And he suddenly leaves without telling me? It gets on my nerves sometimes, especially when there is business to take care of.'

'Don't be harsh, darling. You know Mr Pye that well. We can't ignore the fact that he has been looking unstable for the past few days now. You shouldn't worry him about business, dear.'

'He is the owner and President of Pye —'

'And you are the CEO. How many times has he told you to take and make decisions on your own? *"Young Pye, it's like oil in water, you are the King now. I'm only the advisor"'* Ms Sandati mimicked Richard's voice with the perfection of someone who had heard it for many years.

They both laughed and walked together across the house's foyer.

'Is Mr Zuva around then?' Steve finally asked.

'Mr Zuva?' Ms Sandati stared at him giggling, with her laughing-like eyes. 'Does that man ever go out at all? I've never come across such a person who spends most of his time glued on books rather than eat and enjoy the environment – given the priceless opportunity. Of course, he is at his cottage.'

Steve used one of the house's back doors to visit one of the lovely cottages, which were situated a few hundred or so meters from the house. He knocked softly on the main door and no answer came. Well, it was useless knocking this door anyway. He opened it and was stunned by its current state. There were papers, books, journals, pens, pencils, rulers everywhere in the adjacent living room. The curtains of the room were drawn, pouring in the evening's light. In the far corner of the room was a flat screen TV that showed the National Geographic channel.

An old man sat on the floor at the middle of the room, surrounded by pyramids of hardbacks and half-opened paperbacks, with two laptops on each side. He looked like a modern day Einstein.

'Good morning, or is it afternoon or evening to you, Master Zuva?' Steve greeted politely, afraid that the old man would wake up from the book he was consumed in and snap at him as he had once done a week ago.

The old man was visibly tall and thin, but looked a bit healthy. His eyes were brown like coffee and his hair was a mixture of white and soon-to-be white black hair, the white existing prematurely. The lines that etched his face emphasized that too. It was apparently difficult to estimate his actual age range. After a minute, the man looked up and greeted Steve with a genuine smile.

'Evening, Master Pye. I apologize for the inexcusable state of the room. How was your day?'

The man spoke with the rare quality of a learned person who had experienced and seen a lot in a short period of time.

'It's your space, Master Zuva, not mine to manage,' Steve laughed, thinking of what Ms Sandati would say if she ever visited Master Zuva's cottage. 'My day, by the way, was a hectic one. The lawyers from SteelWorks have grown big heads and President Pye has chosen such a precarious time to disappear. I'm flushed.'

'Master Pye, we are all here for a purpose, a purpose unknown to either you or me, a purpose we might be familiar with, but can't see its true meaning. What is being "cool"? Is it not being cold in a pleasant way, but not very cold?'

Steve shrugged. 'Master Zuva, we are well familiar you are now researching for your possible PhD or something. When you speak to us of such near minds, please, simple words and meanings will do. Thank you!'

Master Zuva guffawed. 'What about telling me what the problem really is and maybe we can find a solution. It's only at times when we realize the reason that makes someone decide to do something whether it is good or indifferent.'

It was now reaching a month and a half since she had saved that tramp and came out of the ordeal with the wallet of the driver of the Mercedes. Rebecca Rocha had thought of going to the police to hand in the wallet and its possessions, but something had made her decide against the idea. She didn't know whether if it was *that*, which made her want to delay the return of the wallet to its owner. The driver's license in it made her see that man's face every day when she was alone and couldn't suppress the urge of looking at it again. Sometimes, she thought that she was becoming obsessed, but her curiosity always got the better of her.

Then there was the money, *one thousand* in neat hundred dollar bills. At frequent intervals, she felt like using the money, only some of it to release the few financial pressures she faced weekly. That amount of money was enough to make her quit her job at the industry and still be able to attend uni the following semester and support her small family. Of course, she would just be borrowing the money like a loan, for she knew that she would be able to repay every cent to that man one day. Another pressing issue was her Grandpa's sudden failing health. She had expensive medicine to buy too.

The only people Rebecca had known as family in her life were her grandparents. She had been told that her parents had both died long ago shortly after her birth. Her grandparents were all she had had for the past twenty years. Although Grandpa had worked as a bureaucrat and had retired with a good pension, it was barely enough to sustain them whilst at the same time paying for a good education. Grandma had been a hard worker, a jack-of-all-trades. It was really hard to remember Grandma crying or being angry. She was always laughing and cheerful in Rebecca's presence, her smiling-laughing-like eyes making her seem like nothing could ever bother her, yet Rebecca knew that sometimes when Grandma was alone, she gave in to the stress and somehow cried to sooth the pain. Their home had been a happy one, and though at first they had moved so often, they had finally settled down on the outskirts of Mbare when Rebecca had started going to high school.

What had always kept her alive and joyful had been the unmatched love her grandparents had showed for each other and her. She was the apple of their eye. And, they had raised her well, into the young woman she had become. God had blessed her with an exceptionally intelligent mind and, for that reason, she was now a third-year medical student who took care of her beloved Grandpa by working part-time at a local steel manufacturing company during her semester holidays. Rebecca could have enjoyed the benefits students in her area of study were privileged to by residing on the campus, but she had declined the offer knowing that if she left home, nobody would be left to take care of Grandpa. Grandma had died in her sleep after Rebecca had turned eighteen and she knew that with her also gone, away from home, Grandpa wouldn't survive for long to leave her a proclaimed orphan.

Resisting the temptation of opening the wallet and looking at the photo on the ID, Rebecca placed it in her safe drawer and shrugged on her working blue overalls. Her hair tied back in a fat ponytail, she went into the small room, which resembled a kitchen and like every morning, prepared the tray of porridge then breakfast for Grandpa. Grandpa usually had his porridge around seven-thirty and tea around ten-thirty. Although he wasn't able to prepare all the essentials by himself, he however could do the little things that were required to complete Rebecca's efforts. As she returned home at lunch from work, breakfast and porridge – including the fruits and snacks she had stacked in the house – settings were just enough to keep Grandpa full before she came back.

If the male personnel, with whom she worked with, knew that she was going to become a qualified doctor of medicine one day, they would have given her more respect and stopped teasing her. Rebecca was the only non-administrative female at the plant and, as she was so accurately attractive even to be considered anything, but an actress or a TV presenter, she had faced a lot of trouble adjusting to the masculine environment during the first days. That was three years ago.

The job was just enough to keep her university tuition, groceries and other necessities coming and it had the advantage of being only two hundred meters away from where she lived after crossing the main road. She simply had to endure these last three weeks and she knew that she would be free then. Med school was going to be attaching her at a local hospital that coming semester. That prospect had its pros and cons, and the cons made her shudder. The attachment meant that she would be required to spend more time away from home, away from Grandpa with no one to substitute her and take care of him giving him the attention a dependent aged person truly desired. She had plans of hiring a temporary maid.

Rebecca's knowledge about the factory had increased over the years. The factory always kept a vacant reserved for her during semester holidays and she figured herself very lucky for jobs weren't that easy to find in such tough times. Her sweet nature had somewhat made her very popular and had protected her from being tasked strenuous jobs, including the few gender pessimists she worked with. She was the favour of the supervisor and a number of co-workers, but that didn't stop some from hating both her and her presence in their male dominated world.

Rebecca's morning shift normally broke at ten for thirty minutes of tea, milk and relief. That day, she found herself engaged in a hot debate about modern day women's dressing. As the only female around, she was the centre of attraction.

'Dress has purpose and occasion, it cannot be more than that,' she said cheerfully.

'And what purpose does one dress in a miniskirt when it's agonizingly cold and windy? What's the purpose there, Miss Rocha?'

'To obviously show off nice legs,' Rebecca smiled. 'If you got them, why not flaunt them to those of the desirable eyes?'

The group of men she sat with at breaks laughed and eyed her admiring her humorous personality. They passed the scones around and drank their milks in more banter.

Minutes later, the factory was brilliantly lit and incredibly noisy. Rebecca crossed the factory floor more than anyone else except the Supervisor did, for she was never assigned to one task for a long period. Thus, she had obtained the ability to learn more and she knew the whole factory like the structure of a human heart. Many of her fellow co-workers had made it a meme to wolf whistle every time she passed by their workstations. At first, it had been very annoying, but she had gotten used to it so much to notice it anymore.

'Hey, Rebecca, how about finishing those cabinet trays for Tom? I have assigned him to go with the manpower to carry the ventilation shafts at the bank,' her supervisor shouted at her over the roar of the machinery. Teatime had just ended ten minutes ago.

'Great, sir!' Rebecca bellowed back and left the machine she was operating to her new assigned post.

A few wolf whistles celebrated her motion. Her mind was already thinking ahead. *Lunchtime*, then leaving the factory for home after a day's work. Panelling the cabinet drawer trays together using a rubber mallet was an easy, but burning task. Fifteen minutes of banging aluminium sheets made her feel filthy and exhausted for the factory turned exceptionally hot at that time of the day owing to the fact that the machines heated up as well from continuous activity. She pulled up a tall stool so she could perch high enough to have access to the workbench and use the mallet without difficulty.

The human noise in the factory seemed to seize suddenly and to her that only meant one thing. The Manager of Production at the company was checking up on progress. They had a deadline of some sort to beat that month and somehow not sweating would have been mistaken for procrastination. Rebecca had met the manager only once on her interview, but she knew his reputation from gossip and that was enough for her to kick the stool aside and appear snowed under. She managed to peek at the direction of the factory's entrance and saw men dressed in immaculate black suits. They all looked like a bunch of bosses taking a tour of the factory, which she later guessed to be true.

The men exchanged business talk, defying the odds of the noise in the factory. Rebecca felt herself tremble a little with anxiety as she sensed them coming in her workstation's direction, possibly towards where the Quality Control Engineers had their offices. She didn't dare look up and maintained her busy-like actions. In the process, she hammered a thin steel sheet so hard that the sheet bent and deformed the whole tray.

'Ms Rocha, for heaven' sake, take it easy!' the Production Manager snapped at her, his voice greatly designed to publicize authority.

Rebecca's ears rang and she felt icy tingles slither down her spine in embarrassment. Her mallet froze in mid-air not knowing what to do next. She didn't dare face the men.

'Ms Rocha? I didn't know you had a lady down here, Mr Huku. That's interesting.'

Behind her, the voice was soft, rich and gentle. It was a foreign voice to her sense data, but something about it made her spin on her heel and turn to face the man who had produced it. Stunned, she stayed absolutely still while her consciousness narrowed down the number of men standing in front of her to only that one man.

'She is the only one, Mr Pye, but she is a hard worker,' the supervisor responded for the manager and winked at an ever-stunned Rebecca. He was sure she had never met Mr Pye before for her expression clearly showed it.

TWO

THE FUNERAL had lasted for only one day and Sue didn't feel like mourning any longer. Tall, light, with long black hair and possessing a glamorous figure, she didn't appear to be the type to cry at funerals, but one who never lost composure.

Suri Hamilton was a charismatic and very attractive girl – that part she knew and was fortunate enough to be told endlessly, especially with her name translating to the Hebrew word for *Princess*. However, she had developed such an immoral reputation for herself in the past to be judged by her appearance. It was at these times of transition that Sue was pleased that she had left the familiar hoods of Borrowdale to live in a quiet, partly inactive suburb called Houghton Park.

She had done it *all*. From dressing slutty, clubbing, drinking, sleeping out, taking school for granted to being titled by the cheapest of names. However, as nasty as she seemed or was rumoured to be, she prided herself for never having smoked or *mated* with anything. Inside, she figured herself to be somewhat pure, but outside she was just too tainted by many complicated memories that would have by no means earned her the title of a saint in a million years of redemption. Her mother hadn't been that beautiful, but pretty in a way that had only been enhanced by her sexy body. Her father was much more of a bulky being than a good-looking man. That blend had produced a rather stunning creature.

Sue had learned to use her outward appearance to her benefit when she had turned into a teenager. She always had boys and men to her manipulation and having a mother who had been a freak for immorality, she had learned it the easy way. Her mother had been a nice lady of the society at the beginning. Sue remembered her that way, and she also remembered what had made her change.

Ned Hamilton was a homosexual who had only married to fulfil his mother's wishes in order to stay inscribed in her will. When Ned had married Chido, Sue's mother, a voluptuous African lady, his mother had threatened to strike him from her will claiming he had offended her pride by marrying a black woman. However, senior Mrs Hamilton had calmed down when Suri was born, and after she died, Ned had inherited his mother's vast fortune without a tear. He had resumed to his old habits from then and had had much pleasure in entertaining young boys than a faithful Chido.

Chido had heard rumours about her husband's infidelity and homosexual cases, but had finally had to see it to believe it. The shock lasted for a few months before she had started to search for her own young men to carry out her plot of retribution. Young Sue had grown up witnessing the different stratagems her parents played, and in confusion, was involved in numerous counts of mischief with hopes of being noticed by them for at least once. That never happened until her mother was diagnosed with HIV.

Chido had used a kitchen knife to slit her wrists open whilst bathing and was human enough to leave a suicide note to her only child. It had said:

I am sorry Suri my love, please forgive me and never replicate my mistakes. Let my weakness be your strength and my downfall be your lesson. Live a healthy and happy life, and know that although I never truly showed it, I love you my daughter.

Ned had realized too late that he too had the deadly virus. Instead of repenting, he had found himself another trophy wife. Being an elegant coloured lady and being called Perrysville, Ned's new wife and Sue's stepmother led by example to her new promisingly gorgeous and fast maturing stepdaughter. Perry had taken Sue out clubbing, to drinking clubs, fashion sprees and all, and Ned seemed to have cared less, but enjoy the little time he had left in secret gay societies and squandering his inheritance.

So rather than mourn her father, Sue had attended the funeral as a mere formality not as a loving daughter. One thing her father had taught her was that *"it was a waste of time to love than to have fun."*

Most of her education had been spent at private colleges and she had clocked the record of going to as many colleges and schools as any girl of her age in a time of five years. How she had managed to pass her Ordinary Levels with perfect grades and at one sitting was only a mystery to her. Her father had made her go to two different schools for her fifth form and she had recently left Dominican Convent High, the latest venture being Arundel School – *Arul*. It was ironic that her father had suffered an irreversible heart failure and died on her very first day at the school. She wondered if she was ever going back there or even to any school.

Now, she was worth three million US dollars plus what her father had left her. She had suddenly discovered from her inherited lawyer that Grandmother Hamilton had been generous enough to leave her a cool two million and another million that was bound in assets the Hamiltons had owned both local and overseas. It was sad enough to note that, after her father who had been the only child – like her – she was the only Hamilton left in her line. If she didn't have kids to inherit that DNA half, the entire line would sadly end with her.

The two guys lingered at the commuter minibus terminus. Shingi was busy secretly caressing his new neighbourhood girlfriend at every opportunity he got. The girl didn't seem to be enjoying it at all, but couldn't do anything about it without causing a scene. She stared at Anesu as if quietly appealing for help. Anesu shrugged and looked away embarrassed. This was a girl whose parents he was well familiar and respected by in the hood. He was sometimes surprised by how fast she had grown.

It was now after a month since that ordeal in the park. As it turned out, Shingi had been turned down by the lady and Anesu's efforts had been practically for nothing else, but becoming good friends with the fellow who had chased him. The lady had liked him too and admired his comical nerve. That had made Shingi even more frustrated, but then Shingi constantly demanded and got the best of everything.

Shingi Rusere was twenty-four years old. He was medium in height, physically sturdy and genetically athletic by nature. He lived with an aunt and three sisters and turned out to be the only male child in the family. His parents worked overseas in Canada and they had left Shingi's aunt to tend for the four children. Shingi's male status made him the head of the house in the absence of Mr Rusere and being a fourth-year veterinary surgeon student at the local university had developed enormous confidence and pride within him, but less in the spectrum of responsibility. At times, Anesu had to deal with his bossiness and hoped that, as time passed, Shingi would grow up. But what Shingi was doing now showed immaturity at its worst. *Was this someone who was smart enough to qualify as a doctor?* It made Anesu want to slap him to wake him up.

The girl kept staring at Anesu, her mouth a thin line of displeasure. *Why didn't I tell him straight away that the reason I dated Shingi was because I thought he would recognize and ask me to become his? After all, every girl in the hood admires him*, she thought sadly, furiously snatching Shingi's hand from her curvy back. *Tell your friend to keep his damned hands to himself, damn it!*

Anesu was torn between telling Shingi to cool it and leaving it alone. After all, this girl knew what she was getting into when she had been stupid enough to enter into Shingi's world. His mother always told him that people usually got what they asked for. Feeling sorry for them was only to worry yourself with business that didn't concern you. But then, his mother had been one of those crazy cases back then.

Anesu Dongo was the only child to Thelma Dongo, then a nineteen-year-old turned single mum. Thelma's father had chased her away from home and her brother had taken her into his care and made her go to college. When she became a qualified architect, Anesu was six years old then. The boy had grown into a tall, simple and charming young man through the years thanks to his mother's well-paying profession.

His mother was a good mentor and a loving one for that matter. She was also strict when it came to manners and how one was supposed to live, especially her son. She had learned from her mistakes and didn't wish to see someone else repeat them. Anesu had grown to be a perseverant character, fuelled by the ambition to make his mother proud and his father curse with regret. In his twenty-three years, his mother had only mentioned his father twice and the message was always the same, *"He just disappeared on me."* That had made the hatred Anesu had for the father he had never met burn like an unending flame. He was now finishing up his fourth and final year at the university, following in his mother's footsteps doing Architectural Science. He was much more at home with setsquares than with the opposite sex and he felt uncomfortable at the way Shingi's girlfriend was staring at him.

'Hey, Shingi,' he whispered.

'What?' Shingi snapped, forcing his hand to penetrate the girl's jacket and pulled it back angrily when the girl furiously pinched it.

'People will start looking now, man. Can't you at least wait till you are alone or something?' Anesu frowned at him.

Shingi ignored him. Anesu shook his head and hoped that a commuter minibus would pick them up soon. He could glimpse anger slowly developing in the girl's eyes as Shingi stubbornly pursued with his undesired gestures. A scene was going to develop soon, that was definite. He was about to move away when someone suddenly prod his arm from behind. Shortly filled with anxiety, he swung around apprehensively.

Sue couldn't believe what she was seeing. *Was this a coincidence?*

'Er – is there anyone behind you, in the queue, I mean?' she asked shyly. It was a pretty silly question considering that there was barely an ordinary queue existing.

Anesu examined her thoroughly and instantaneously felt his feet float. He remembered where he had seen her before and the oddness of the occasion made him want to laugh. His eyes gleamed instead. Up close, the girl in her neat uniform looked alluring. He was still trying to get his breath back.

'Now, I think there is,' he smiled at her.

Sue beamed. He still had that mysterious voice that exuded charm and affability. She was normally cool and operative around guys of all sorts, but she momentarily felt like a bubbling idiot. The guy wasn't extremely handsome or all that, but he was good looking enough to make any lady be interested. It wasn't his looks that generally made him enchanting. It was something to do with his eyes and the way they looked at her. There was no lust or purpose in them.

They looked as if they were laughing at an unsaid joke, and mostly a mixture of kindness, care and respect for those they scanned. She felt genuinely silly. On no account in her life had she felt like this. It was as if someone had lit a green candle inside her heart.

Anesu waited for her to say something, but she didn't seem like she was going to. He had seen many beautiful girls before, but it was either their hair made them beautiful or their bodies or simply their clothes. What was in front of him was pure beauty, natural beauty. The girl was all fine, but Anesu had self-studied enough psychology to make him cautious. The girl was drop dead gorgeous, but he didn't like the self-confidence he foresaw in her. It was of a person who exactly knew the way she looked and that was always dangerous.

'I'm sorry, but your uniform, it looks…' Anesu began. 'I could swear I have seen you before, in a Convent uniform. However, you, my lady, look pretty all the same.'

Sue smiled. 'Thanks, I changed schools,' she said, eyes full on him.

Anesu smiled back. 'Interesting that, hope your app number stays the same. I'm Anesu and what is your app number, my lady?'

Sue looked at him eyes wide open with amusement. This guy didn't fail to amaze. That was one pick up line she had never come across before. 'I thought you'd want to know my name first, Anesu, and yet you ask for my number,' she said creamily, rolling her eyes.

'I only need your number. You can keep it if you don't want with it.'

Fazed, Sue gave in and said her number out loud. She was more disappointed when he didn't even record it down. He just stared at her.

What a queer dude, she thought.

After some time still at Arundel School, she was finding life a little bit demanding now. Her stepmother was always out and about, and Sue had found it odd that she didn't enjoy going out anymore, but to stay at home on weekends either sleeping or watching TV. She guessed that her father had somewhat died with another part of her. The idea of being an orphan hadn't surfaced in her head until one day when one of her school buddies had asked her if she had any relatives living close by.

When their kombi came, Anesu found himself separated from Sue by Shingi and his girlfriend. Shingi had given up on her, and was now trying to make conversation with Sue. Sue tried to be polite and answered some of Shingi's questions. She had enough experience to detect the smell of alcohol from Shingi's breath and so had to keep her nose at a safe distance. However, her gaze kept resting on Anesu three seats from her. The guy didn't even show the slightest awareness that she was there and that she had just given him her number. She felt herself getting angry with him.

Why did he act so cold? Didn't he feel the attraction between them?

Shingi caught her glancing at Anesu and grimaced. He refocused his attention at his girlfriend and tried to apologize, but the girl had had enough. She had taken being fondled on a kombi's queue very personal. She didn't even show any sign of acknowledging Shingi's presence beside her. Shingi ended up producing his phone – after plugging earphones into his ears – closed his eyes, and leaned back in his seat.

Anesu was busy meditating, staring out of the window as the kombi traversed the roads. Suddenly, he felt his left hand being grasped and Shingi's girlfriend's fingers locked firmly on his. Shocked, he looked back at her, then at Shingi. Shingi was far away in dreamland, eyes closed and ears blazed by melodies. Anesu looked at the girl and saw her direct a breath-taking smile at him. She squeezed his hand passionately. Not knowing how to react, he smiled and squeezed the hand back.

The joy that the girl felt was too intense that she seemed to glow, her smile lighting her up like a golden angel. For the first time since they had boarded the kombi, Anesu found himself looking at the lady whose number he had stacked in his memory. Sue was glaring at him like she wanted to murder him. It was evident that she had seen the exchange of affection between him and his best friend's girl. He looked away unconcerned.

Three

STEVE'S EYES were so open, amused, his voice so cool and deliberate for a mouth that was forever smiling. He couldn't really believe his luck. He thought of all those weeks he had spent searching, only to find out that day that what he had been searching for was all along under his very nose. It was unbelievable, so unthinkable. God had truly heard his prayers.

Had God truly answered her prayers? Rebecca admired the enormous office with genuine curiosity. The portraits of former Presidents of Pye Industries were nailed at one wall in a systematic line. She watched Steve rise slowly from behind an enormous desk and gesture toward a pair of armchairs, which were before a fireplace in one corner of the office. Rebecca hesitated for her overalls, although clean, weren't in a state to acquaint with the silky material of the chairs.

'Please, sit. I've been dying to see you since our brief meeting last month. It's been an unusual necessity, Ms Rocha, I presume?' Steve smiled.

'I can't believe it. You actually remember me?' Rebecca managed to say. 'It's been long, and – Wow, you are Steven Marlow, my boss, I presume.'

'Correction, Ms Rocha. Firstly, I am Steven Pye. Richard Pye is my father, that's your boss.'

'But, but –' rather animatedly, Rebecca refused to believe him. 'But your name is Marlow, how can it be Pye too?'

Steve stared at her surprised. 'You know my mother's maiden name, but how?'

Rebecca blushed, remembering his wallet. 'Well, you sort of dropped your particulars that day. I thought you had noticed.'

'Oh,' Steve's tone was controlled. 'I thought I had been robbed. So you still have the wallet?'

'Yes, I still do.'

'And the cash in it? You used some of course, I shouldn't have asked. Sorry.'

Rebecca's forehead wrinkled. 'I used nothing. Everything is just as it was, Mr Pye. Why would I use your money?'

'I guessed in your kind of situation –'

'My kind of situation, Mr Pye? What do you take me for?' Rebecca stared hard at him, annoyed mostly.

'I just meant that, the money in it was a lot, anyone could have used it.'

'I never use what's not rightfully mine or something that I haven't been given. I'm sorry to disappoint you, sir, but no matter how bad my situation is, I live by my own principals.'

'I'm sorry if you took it the wrong way, it's just that people nowadays tend to –' Steve said defensively.

Rebecca frowned openly. '*People nowadays?* You act as if you aren't one of *people*, aren't you human? I didn't use your money and I'll bring your wallet tomorrow, sir. Goodbye!'

Steve realized that she had left the room after a while. His throat got raw with emotion. He shook his head.

'Now how can I be so stupid and meaningless? Why did I say that for?' he said sullenly to himself.

He had only found her to lose her again. He had hoped for a better start and this wasn't what he had in mind. *All for a bloody wallet and some money.*

Moments later, Steve sat in his office reading a file from the employees' records courtesy of his secretary. She was called Rebecca and she was currently the only on-the-floor female factory worker at the company. Twenty-one years of age, guardian was stated as her grandfather who had the surname Rocha as well. Rebecca's granddad was probably her father's father. What really made his eyes pop out was her academic qualifications record. He couldn't believe his eyes once more. *Was this record prepared correctly, was it authentic? What was such a beautiful lady studying to become a doctor doing in a factory?*

He was tempted to jot down her home address, go out to find and ask her, but he knew that it was better off if he let her cool down and possibly do it whenever she returned to see him. She had promised to return his wallet the next day and Rebecca didn't seem like the sort who would go back on her word.

Rebecca walked furiously across the industry's wide road, impatient to reach home as soon as possible. Steven Pye had such nerve. How could he accuse her of using his money? Principally, she was even more seethed by the fact that she had made inaccurate perceptions. Steve Pye was just like all the other self-centred males who thought best of themselves and less of women, *the brats!* How could she have been so actually blind to think he was different? Her mind was so preoccupied that she bumped into someone and barely looked up, but cursed loudly.

'Hey, lady, you were the one who stepped into me. Why snap at me? Are you having your *period?*' a voice came.

Rebecca looked up and wondered if the man behind the voice really meant it. Thinking of Steve, she frowned.

'No need to frown at me, but hey keep it up. You look eccentric that way, please frown some more.'

Is this guy serious? Rebecca thought glaring at him. He was standing in her way, so she gave him an indignant *"move aside"* look.

'I'm not letting you pass until you apologize. Come on, grimace...' and *snap!* The guy held a phone with a camera. He took another photo of her frowning.

'What's your problem?' Rebecca did snap.

'My problem is when birds like you lose their manners. My mother would surely spank you. You look like you have had a rough day. Anything bad that can't be fixed by a smile?' the guy said sweetly.

'Are you for real?'

The guy smiled either way. 'I'm sure I'm not fiction, are you?'

'Can you please leave me alone? I don't want –'

'You don't want to smile? Well, I got news for you lovely one, I'm gonna be like an unwanted bug till you smile, just once. I'm sure you won't poop anything if you do. Come on, you know you want to, smile, smile, smile pretty one.'

Rebecca wanted to swear at him, but somehow she just couldn't master enough courage to do so. She gave it to the dude. He had a way with words. Her smile gave her away.

'Ahhh, yes, you smiled. Can I walk you? I can smile for you if you want, only that without your kind of face, I'll look more like a cartoon.'

That broke the spell and Rebecca found herself giggling. 'I can very much walk myself home. Thanks anyway.'

'You owe me, lady. You bumped into me, so in return you'll pay me back by letting me walk you home, and that isn't for negotiation. Did I tell you that you look good in that *overall?*'

It was something about the guy's confidence and crazy charm that prevented her from chasing him away.

'Who are you? You are one character I have never come across. You are funny, very funny and weird.'

The guy beamed and held out his hand. 'The name is Dongo, Anesu Dongo,' he said in a James Bond like manner.

Rebecca laughed and shook his hand. 'I'm Rebecca, or should I say Rocha, Rebecca Rocha.'

Anesu couldn't believe he was doing this. He was supposed to be running an errand for his uncle. His uncle wanted him to deliver a sensitive confidential document to the CEO of Pye Industries personally. A major hustler was what his uncle was, but Anesu didn't know what he really did for a living. However, his uncle was a rich man and Anesu was deeply grateful to him. His uncle had been there for his mother when nobody had wanted her.

Anesu had bumped into Rebecca unexpectedly and the lady had attracted him enough to make him derail from his purposeful route. If his uncle could see him now, he was sure that though his uncle was an amiable man, he would have a word or two to say because the document he was supposed to deliver was of high priority.

'So, Becky, where from and where to?'

The question was so direct, but she didn't mind. 'I'm coming from work to my home. What about you?'

'From town to Pye Industries offices playing messenger for my uncle,'

'Wow.'

'Wow you too, lady. Where do you work?'

'Pye Industries.'

'You must be kidding, right?' Anesu said eyebrows up. 'Do you know the CEO, Mr Pye? I'm going to see him.'

Rebecca faltered. 'Well, a little. So where are you going now?'

'I'm walking you home, my lady. What does it look like I am doing?' Anesu smiled at her.

'It seems like you are trying your luck. I'm sorry to disappoint you, but I'm not interested,' Rebecca said firmly.

'You are not interested? On what, actually? You have lost me.'

Rebecca looked up at him and saw surprise. She knew that it was faked – play acted. Nevertheless, this guy was good. He must have knocked quite a number of ladies off their feet with such smoothness. Some sort of player perhaps.

'Come on now, I'm not stupid.'

'And whoever said you were? Do you think I'd hit on a lady wearing an overall? Please, God, help me!'

Rebecca fumed with anger. It was now twice that day within an hour she had been openly offended. *What is it with this gender?* She thought heatedly. *They are all bastards!*

'Please go, now!'

Anesu laughed. 'I thought we were getting to know each other, Becky. How can you take me seriously? You have probably been hit on by a thousand guys, telling you that you are gorgeous, beautiful, etc. You are too much for a dude like me. I prefer my eggs pretty, but not excessively pretty – but it wouldn't hurt to be friends, would it? From a stranger to a beautiful stranger, let's become friends, please.'

'Dude, I just met you. For all I know you could be a –'

'A serial killer, a rapist, a *tsola*, or wait…' Anesu was smiling as he spoke, '…worse, a player.'

Rebecca laughed shaking her head. 'A player is worse than a serial killer?'

'To some, yes indeed. Definitely indeed, spooky, but true. Friends?'

Rebecca looked him directly in the eyes and believed that this was no ordinary guy. *Was she seeing right? What was it she had felt for Steve?*

All in all, though, as Anesu suspended his hand for her to shake in agreement, she found herself liking the way he went about himself. You could tell when he was bluffing or not, joking or serious. She shook the hand and felt an indescribable feeling of finding something new.

'Yay! So you finished school when? I'm at Harare International University doing Architectural Science – final year, sorry to brag.'

'I can't say that I actually finished school, like not yet. Hey, you said you are at HIU?' Rebecca was enthusiastic.

'Yes, why? You know someone there?'

'I learn there.'

Anesu was bewildered. 'You are at HIU too? But you said you work at Pye Industries.'

'So?' Rebecca enjoyed the confusion that showed on his face. 'Isn't it possible to do the two? We are still on holiday, aren't we?'

'Well, I...,' Anesu stammered. 'You must be a busy girl. What are you into at HIU then? I haven't seen you before when I visit the *greens*.'

'What are *greens*?' Rebecca was a bit confused.

'You learn at HIU and you don't know what a *green* is?' Anesu laughed. 'Places where you find girls relaxing, where dudes go out to hunt for some love or lust.'

Rebecca giggled. 'Oh, guess I wouldn't know. I'm rarely on the main campus except during exams.'

Anesu now looked very confused. 'I don't understand how that is possible. Are you like a part-time student?'

'I am a full-time. We learn at the Medical School near Pari, the hospital. I am doing medicine. Three years running, and two to go,' she grinned broadly.

Thirty minutes later, Rebecca prepared her grandpa's lunch in a good mood. She laughed every time she thought of the look on Anesu's face when she had told him about her studies. He had looked utterly stunned and sceptic. She wondered if she was going to see him again. He had seemed like such an odd, but lovable character.

Ms Dongo looked in the direction of the kitchen with outmost interest. *What had gotten into him now? Had she fed him too much philosophy?*

'And may I ask why you suddenly want to spend the rest of your semester holiday working at Pye Industries? Was it your uncle's idea?'

'No, Mum, I just need to get some feel of steel,' Anesu responded aloud from the kitchen that night doing the dishes whilst Ms Dongo sat with her feet on the sofa in the sitting room, relaxing after what seemed to have been a busy day.

'Why not the bank? I could have easily found something there for you, dear.'

'I want to construct factories someday, Mum, not banks. Anyway, I need to be involved in some real physical work. Paper and all makes me groggy. My attachment at your bank last year really sucked.'

'Hey, little man, don't insult my work place,' Ms Dongo laughed. 'So how are you going to get employed there? Let me guess, your uncle?'

'Guess again. I spoke to the CEO today whilst running an errand for uncle and he said I could start tomorrow if I want to. We have become buddies,' Anesu informed her.

'Friends with Steven Pye? Now you are growing immense moral fibre. I can't say I am surprised. You know where you got those genes, right?'

They laughed the statement away.

Sue spent her days in a pensive mood. That *guy* hadn't called and she had expectantly searched for him at the bus terminus daily with no luck.

The girls at her school had welcomed her like a Queen, and she had adopted well enough than she had anticipated. She had a well-known reputation in the youthful society thanks to social media platforms such as *hello.com*, *Twitter*, *Facebook* and *Instagram*. Many had expected her to act likewise at school.

However, much to her surprise, school had suddenly become interesting and serious. Their teachers were professionals and they worked them to the extent where it was impossible to be involved with anything else, but books. Long ago, she could have complained to her father and she could have been transferred to another school of her own choice just like that, but Arundel High had unexpectedly stuck in her system. It was a mystery how her father had actually managed to get her into the school. Sue never wished of leaving it until she finished school.

For once, she felt the need to settle down. What she couldn't understand though was why she couldn't forget Anesu and why he had affected her so much. Her heart ached for him to call. He didn't even know her name and that had made her bitter. She had however seen Shingi a couple of times, but had decided against asking him about Anesu's whereabouts. Something in her warned her that it would give results, but it wouldn't be the best of ideas.

Four

ANESU COULDN'T grasp why Shingi was suddenly so uptight. It was on countless occasions when Anesu ignored the damnable signs that were slithering up as of late.

Shingi was shimmering, bubbling with rare impulses of someone who was possibly on drugs. They had grown up together in a quiet neighbourhood that it made it difficult to envision where Shingi had caught the habit. At seven in the morning, his friend was already looking informally fidgety. Like usual, Shingi spent most of his time in town during semester holidays. The two were momentarily in a commuter minibus, en route the CBD.

'Why do you have to do this, man? Have you become a sucker for steel?' Shingi asked in a sarcastic tone.

'Conductor, please drop me off around the second junction to the factories!' Anesu shouted. 'It's a better way to end my holiday man,' he said to Shingi, getting ready to get off the kombi.

'We all know it's not about the money.'

'I rarely am motivated by money to do things. You of all people should know that,' Anesu responded smiling at a young lady who was in a suit, sitting at his side, probably on her way to work. She smiled back at him as he handed her her change from the conductor.

'Enjoy your day, Architect Dongo,' Shingi laughed ironically.

'You too, Animal Doctor Rusere.'

Anesu walked slowly towards Pye Industries trying to figure out why he was doing this exactly. In the past, he had had glimpses of crazy, but this was beyond anything crazy he had ever done.

What am I doing here? He quizzed himself.

It was going to be a lifetime experience working at the factory. He went straight to the Production Manager's office and was introduced to the factory's supervisor. After that, he was provided with a new overall that looked too big for him, leather gloves and a pair of black hard leather industrial boots.

Within thirty minutes of being shown what he was supposed to be doing and not, he was assigned to working on cutting metal sheets using a huge scary, but apparently harmless machine. The job was to insert metal sheets into the machine where they were cut into the appropriate halves.

It was nearly two hours later when he realized what he was doing and where he was. All his concentration had been focused on the machine in fear of operating it the wrong way and messing up a sheet in the process. An experienced middle-aged factory worker watched from a distance, overseeing Anesu's work and safety as he was new. Anesu's eyes watered inside the safety goggles he wore and he could feel his palms extra sweaty within his new leather gloves.

'Sir, are you finished with those? Mr Dindi sent me to get them. He wants to punch the hinge holes on them now,' a sweet voice interrupted him.

Anesu carefully switched off the machine and looked back. He took off his goggles and produced an ambitious grin.

Rebecca stood there frozen by shock. *Was she seeing correctly?*

'Anesu!' she gaped. 'Anesu?'

'Ahhh, you remembered my name. So stimulating,' Anesu took off his left glove to wipe the sweat off his face.

'I don't believe this. I've never seen you here before,' Rebecca was entirely confused. 'You work here? How – I am positive you don't work here, but –'

'It's because I'm enjoying my first day here, ma'am. I couldn't think of any other way of seeing you again, so I persuaded Mr Pye to employ me.'

'You mean to say that you looked for work here just to see me? Are you crazy?' Rebecca was stunned.

'I am, but hey, it's fun. It's exuberating to the bone,' Anesu boasted. It was not, he was putting on a brave face. It hurt like hell.

Rebecca was lost off thoughts. She couldn't gage if this guy was truly nuts or somehow a great unpredictable human being. She felt an odd rise of affection for him and tried to suppress it.

'I didn't know architects were physical people. I thought you were lazy, drawing stuff for people and letting them do all the hard work whilst you sip coffee in your plush offices.'

Anesu laughed. He hadn't perceived Rebecca to possess such a sense of humour, but her smiling-like eyes should have warned him. 'A medical doctor at a steel factory, now that's just as funny too, don't you think?'

Rebecca blushed. So, he remembered, yet he was now unshaken.

'Hey, Ms Rocha, I have been waiting for those sheets for ages now. What's keeping you?' a short squat man with enormous gorilla like arms came walking towards them. He looked and he was apparently short tempered.

'Sorry, Mr Dindi, I was just bringing them now,' Rebecca jumped.

'Sorry doesn't give me anything. Hurry now, I want them now,' the man was as mean as he looked. The distaste he had for Rebecca truly showed in his eyes.

'I'll bring them for you, sir. It's my fault, I hadn't finished cutting them,' Anesu intervened, going over to load them over a mobile trolley.

'You do your job, young man. I want Ms Rocha to do it as I asked her to long ago. I can't have a lazy little girl working under my factory,' Mr Dindi snapped at him.

'With all due respect, Mr Dindi, is it? Last time I checked, the name Pye Industries, not Dindi Industries was inscribed at the gate, Mr Dindi,' Anesu said so calmly and so annoyingly. He said it as if he was offering someone ice cream or a drink.

Rebecca and the other workers who were witnessing the drama couldn't believe Anesu's nerve. Rebecca's heart beat faster, scared, anticipating Mr Dindi possibly reacting in a physical manner.

Luckily, she didn't find out for she heard the supervisor call her name.

'There you are, Ms Rocha. Mr Pye wants to see you pronto, get moving.'

Rebecca entered the office feeling very uneasy. In her hand, she held the leather wallet, ready to dispose it. Steven Pye was there waiting patiently.

Her heart skipped a beat. He looked more ravishing in a black suit and white shirt knotted by a blue silk tie. She remembered their last meeting and her face darkened.

'I am a fool at times, Ms Rocha, and yesterday I slipped and publicized it to you. I'm truly sorry about what I said yesterday,'

Steve said quietly, in a voice that made Rebecca want to cry for no apparent reason. She blinked foolishly. 'Thank you for coming, Ms Rocha, I thought you'd refuse to after the way I treated you.' His gaze was steady all the way. 'I was wondering if you'd forgive my silliness.'

'Here is your wallet, Mr Pye, as I promised you. Can I leave, now? After all, that was what you wanted,' Rebecca's tone was firm – it even surprised her.

Steve felt his heart sink. His nerves were in shreds and he wasn't sure how much more of Rebecca's refusal to compromise he could stand without getting frustrated.

'That's not the only thing I want. In fact, keep the cash. Just give me back the ID,' he said lamely.

'And why would you let me have all that cash for?' Rebecca frowned at him.

Steve was lost of words. He avoided looking straight at her. 'It's clear you surely need it more than I do,' he finally said.

Rebecca's eyes bulged. This was outrageous. 'You are unbelievable, Mr Pye. The money I am only getting from you is the salary that is rightfully mine. I don't want your money. Yesterday you were complaining about how I must have used your money for my own needs, and now when I give it back to you untouched, you say you don't want it asking me to take it. Just how much pride do you possess, Mr Pye, seriously?'

'Ms Rocha, I didn't –'

'Mr Pye, I think I gave you back what's yours as it was when you unfortunately lost it. So, please, can I go?' Rebecca's fury intensified by the word.

Minutes later, Steven stared out of the window into the sun and wondered where he had gone wrong exactly. Intelligent ladies were truly a *problem*. Everything he had said had been translated and misinterpreted. *How could he tell Rebecca then just how he felt about her now without her perceiving it as something bad?*

He badly needed advice, but couldn't think of anyone to ask. The name Mr Zuva finally bloomed in his mind.

'You got issues with Mr Pye,'

'What?' Rebecca woke from her daydreaming.

Anesu was walking her home for the second time from work, the only difference now being that they were now co-workers and wore overalls in the heat. He was returning to work to resume his job with the others. He had discovered that only Rebecca had a special arrangement at the factory to leave at lunch for some reason he was yet to discover.

'Ever since you returned from the CEO's office, you have been looking apprehensive. More like a reformed Mr Dindi,' Anesu said smoothly.

Rebecca found herself giggling, the tension in her waning. 'I have seen that you have won over the old man. How did you do that? You must be a genius.'

She had been stunned when she had returned to the factory floors from another heated one on one with Steven Pye and straight to tea to see Anesu exchanging jokes with Mr Dindi. Mr Dindi had even broken a personal record by giving her a weak smile and a kind nod.

Just what kind of a gift did this dude have that made people give in to his irresistible charm? Resting and having a chat with Grandpa, Rebecca was astonished when she remembered all the information she had spilled about herself to Anesu that afternoon.

'You are smiling, now that's a nice picture to see. It can easily entertain me to sleep better and forget my rheumatism,' Grandpa said leaning over his rocking armchair, watching the sinking orange sun from their little veranda. 'I used to do that every time I thought of your grandma when we were still *vapfana.*'

Rebecca hadn't been aware that she was smiling. All she had in her mind was Anesu's free-floating banter. However, it wasn't a good sign smiling subconsciously.

'Just thinking about this comedy I saw yesterday on TV, Grandpa, nothing else,' she said flipping over a module about Diagnostics.

'Old, but human as well, my dear. Old, but human,' Grandpa said wisely.

'Now what is that supposed to mean, Grandpa?' she asked smiling, not looking at him in fear of betraying her thoughts.

Grandpa laughed in an aged voice. 'I think you know what I mean, you only need to understand it, nothing else.'

When Rebecca dreamt exchanging wedding vows with Steven Pye in a white wedding setting that night, she woke up sweating as if she had been having a nightmare.

Steve was anxious as he drove away from SteelWorks' driveway.

How could he have forgotten the proposed agreement documents between Pye Industries and SteelWorks at home at such a crucial day? This Rebecca issue wasn't to be underestimated for it was affecting him more than he had wanted to admit.

"Talk to her and listen without talking." Only those seven words were what Mr Zuva had offered him as help. Mr Zuva had refused to shed more light on them claiming that, deep inside, Steve already knew their meaning.

The signing of the deal was going on at nine o'clock that morning thanks to Mr Zuva's rich advice. He wished that his father hadn't given him the praise for something that wasn't genuinely his. Steve hadn't told him that it had all been Mr Zuva's careful critical thinking that had given him the skill to persuade the SteelWorks directors to be acquired by Pye Industries over a reasonable price.

Sue was mad at her phone. It hadn't even warned her that its battery was soon to be flat. Thus, it had gone dead around midnight and the result was her waking up at quarter past seven. She hadn't even bathed for she knew that she was late for school already. On the other hand, her stepmother had spent four days away, but informed her every night on her whereabouts, which was having continuous fun at a friend's house.

Sue was often scared of aggravated burglary during the nights she was alone, but three days after, she became too tired to think about it. School was working her overtime, she barely had time to watch TV, relax or even think of getting robbed in the middle of the night.

Sue was looking forward to the weekend, but now she had other worries. No kombis were around and those which passed by were already packed to accommodate her. She began to wave for private cars as well, desperate. The idea of getting herself a car really appealed to her more than ever.

The *car* slowed down and stopped in front of her. She didn't have a choice, but to ask for a lift. The passenger's window slid down electronically.

'Can you please give me a lift to town, I'm in a hurry.'

'Sure, hop in.'

Gratefully, she inserted herself in. She had numerous experience of sliding upfront in men's cars, so to her it didn't seem odd or anything – in school uniform or not. There were those who looked on and muttered to themselves, but she cared less. She examined the driver fully for the first time and held her gaze and breath. *Wow!*

'You learn at Arundel, right?' the driver said.

'Yes,' Sue said not able to take her eyes off him, 'and I am so late, the Madam will give me a ticking or two, my first time though,' she added smiling broadly.

'Your first time, hey, so you must be a prompt good girl then?'

'Most naturally,' Sue giggled, finally taking her eyes off him. 'It's just that I am new.'

'I'm off to Mount Pleasant. I pass by your school's road every day otherwise I wouldn't have stopped for I'm in a bit of a hurry myself Miss…'

'Sue.'

'Ms Sue, nice surname, Ms Sue.'

'No, Sue is my first name. I am Suri Hamilton and I believe that you must be Mr Pye's son of Pye Industries,' Sue said intelligently without being clever.

Steven's eyes came from the road anxiously to hers. 'You know who I am?' he floundered in speech, stunned.

'Obviously, who wouldn't, Mr Pye? You are a well-known figure – the media and all,' Sue explained without taking her eyes off him this time.

She couldn't wait to reach school and brag about having been given a ride by Steven Pye, one of the dazzling wealthy eligible bachelors in the country.

To Steven, Sue looked far beyond her age. She portrayed the graceful, enticing structure of a girl who was growing into a stunning lady. And hell, she wasn't shy, which was pretty clear. He could feel her eyes scanning him, and he was uneasy for the long term of the drive. They exchanged casual banter along the way, Sue doing most of the talking. It took Steve about thirty minutes to reach Mount Pleasant. He turned into Arundel Road, toward the school.

'I don't know how to thank you, Mr Pye. I'm roughly on time,' Sue said thankfully, as Steve parked his car along the road's sideway where cars came and went, dropping off students.

'Call me Steve, ma'am, and please don't thank me, it was the least I could do.'

'And what more could, can you do?' Sue narrowed her eyes, smiling at him.

The question took Steve completely off-guard. His head was in a state of undeniable confusion. This young lady truly knew how to cause tremors in men, and he wondered if it was the how-many-eth time she had done it. It was clear that it wasn't her first using flattery.

'I could give you a call if you give me your phone number, which is if you wish,' Steve found himself saying. He bit his lips so ashamed of his conduct. *What the hell am I doing asking for a phone number from a schoolgirl?* He cursed himself.

Sue expertly took a small notepad from her blazer's pocket together with an expensive looking pen. She scribbled her number on a page and sweetly tore it off. Giving him yet another unsettling smile, she handed it over.

'I'll be waiting for your call, and thanks for the ride,' she said, smoothly caressing Steve's left cheek with her baby soft-like hand. She got out and dashed for the school without looking back.

Steve didn't move for exactly a minute. He was completely paralyzed and his cheek had turned slightly pink at the spot where Sue's palm had brushed it.

In the past few years, he had been intimate with not more than three dashing, beautiful ladies. They were all successful, came from wealthy families, and what many would call marriage material. Those relationships had only lasted for a year at best and three months the least. They had lacked reality, filled with tendencies that were more superficial.

That day, in only a few minutes, he had experienced something he had never known existed and it was all because of an eighteen or rather seventeen-year-old girl. He didn't know if it was a blessing in disguise that he had forgotten those documents at home just to meet Miss Hamilton or a curse. Shrugging himself back to reality, he smiled bleakly and stuffed Sue's number into his pocket.

Five

THE DYNAMIC principle of existence was indeed survival. And the reward of survival was supposed to be pleasure, wasn't it? Then why was *she* feeling so guilty, so misjudged by the considerate pattern of the reactive mind and the compulsive emotions that seemed to embrace her at the most unappealing of times?

When her phone rang, she leapt with joy as she saw the incoming caller's identity foreign to her phonebook's data. Ten in the night, trying to prepare for an upcoming test, Sue had only her nerves to fight with.

'Hello,' she answered in a seductive tone, playing with the stray strands of her long hair.

'Did you miss me?'

The voice ignited her memory. Although it wasn't the one she had been expecting to hear, she felt her heart pulsate with excitement. 'Did I ever? And now you call me after all this time. What took you so long? Did you mess up my digits in that brain of yours?'

'My mind's reservoir is perfectly, patiently rich, thank you. It happens that I did take my time, to make you a little bit nervous, setting off your fuses. I doubt if you remember me now.'

'Anesu, how can I forget? The dude who hits on his friend's girl in his presence. Hilarious, really,' Sue giggled.

Anesu paused in breath for a while from the other end fascinated by the fact that the girl could remember his name of all things. 'She likes me. What am I supposed to do? Hazel blames me for her connection with Shingi, and it may well have been my fault. I can't simply blame her, be oblivious of her feelings,' he defended himself.

Such a nice guy, Sue thought grinning. *No wonder this Hazel has a crush on him.* 'I like you too,' she said at whim, without thinking at all.

Anesu was mentally quirked for a few seconds. He resisted the idea of it and was subject to Sue's remark in an understanding kind of way. That was the first time a girl had ever said that so openly to him. He was awed by her boldness.

'Is that a fact, Suri Hamilton?'

'What? What did you just call me?' Sue was truly shocked.

'I'm talking to Suri Hamilton, aren't I?' Anesu said consciously aware of the reaction he had caused. 'Don't tell me that you have now forgotten your name.'

'How do you know my name, Anesu? Have you been spying on me?' Sue demanded. One thing she was certain of was that she hadn't given him her name and he had annoyingly never asked for it. *How could he know?*

Anesu laughed warmly. 'The basic nature of wise men, Sue dear, is to observe what they see instead of just seeing.'

'That doesn't answer my question. How do you know my name?'

'In this world of tech and gadgets, you really have to ask me how? Come on now, Sue, I thought you learned at Arundel,' Anesu said confidently.

Sue grinned. She had an idea where he had found her name. But then *how* was still the question. 'What does my school have to do with it?'

'You girls from Arul have a habit.'

'A habit of what, Anesu? I hate begging for answers.'

'I never took you for a beggar. You don't look like it anyway with all that money gleaming on you.'

Sue was maddened by this potentially offensive statement. 'Am I to apologize for my grandmother leaving me money? Is it a sin to be a little fortunate?'

'A little fortunate?' Anesu snorted and giggled producing a rather odd tone. 'What is a little fortunate to you, Sue dear? Do you know how expensive it is to learn at Convent or Arundel? Funny thing, you have been to both within a term. A little fortunate you must be,' he expressed.

'True values of happiness, bearable existence, apathy and anger aren't within men's total control, Anesu. If I am born in a family with money, can I be accountable for someone who was born in poverty? Living a pleasant and hopeful life in general is what everyone desires, but do we all live pleasant and hopeful lives whether we have got money or not?'

Those words had him thinking. It had been risky to test her, but he had got what he hadn't even thought of receiving. Anesu had estimated Sue to defend herself and become angry with him, but she was as cool as a cold drink of Pepsi.

'Are you still there, Anesu?'

'Yes – yes,' Anesu chocked off his sudden dry throat. This meant trouble. His heart was being pulled in two different directions. 'I was just thinking of how many beautiful ladies, like yourself, have an intelligent mind such as yours, Sue. I am impressed.'

'How about if I impress you more in person, do you care to meet again, hey?' Sue went for it.

Nobody had ever called her *intelligent* before. Maybe the words freaky, smart, beautiful and sexy would come out, but not the word intelligent. What made it more appealing was that it was a genuine compliment.

'Name the place and time, your call,' Anesu listened whilst Sue gave him her plans for the meet.

"I will be in town around two-three," Rebecca had said to him. It was a nice Friday glistened by the late stages of winter and the initial stages of summer. The skies threatened to open the heavens and produce rains, but for now, it was sunny and partly cloudy. Anesu salvaged the anticipation of meeting her. It was his first week at Pye Industries and it had enthused pretty well. Rebecca was really something. She had surprised him by showing off her humorous side more than often and he somewhat felt more attracted to her. All he had seen her in were her overalls. He only contemplated on how she would look in casual wear.

'It's half two, man, where is this person you want to meet?' Shingi was getting impatient.

He was almost his normal self that day, but looked a bit jumpy like someone craving for a small dosage of an addictive substance. They were only a few weeks from going back to college and Anesu thought it as the main reason why Shingi was cutting down the pleasure for his courses started two weeks earlier.

The two were waiting at the rendezvous point and nothing that looked like the *person* they were waiting for was in sight. Anesu's back was aching, still fresh from the factory. He hoped that the oil he had been working with that day hadn't transferred some of its odour onto his skin. Coming from lunch from Pye Industries at one-thirty hadn't given him enough time to sneak home and bath. Whatever state he was in, he didn't worry much.

When the lady walked towards them, she did look devastatingly stunning in clothes. Anesu felt dumb at the sight of her. Somehow, she had a simple skirt and white t-shirt beneath a pink velvet jacket. Her skirt wasn't body-hugging, neither was it loose, but reaching her knees, it was enticingly hiding what could be nothing, but great long legs. Her complexion radiated her attire in a most delicious manner. Anesu glanced at Shingi and couldn't blame him for suddenly acting like a retard.

She walked over to them and gave Anesu an unexpected hug. Anesu felt his feet go weak like jelly was their texture. He could barely breathe. They rarely knew each other and yet she was hugging him tight like a long lost friend. She smiled amiably at Shingi and judging from Shingi's expression, he looked a bit odd at the fact that he hadn't received a hug too from this *angel*.

'Took your time, didn't you, Sue?' Anesu enjoyed her looks with all might and under. Who else could be as lucky as he?

'I didn't go to school today. It's our *exeat weekend*, so I had a tough time catching a ride. I only realized later that I should have invited you to my house instead of meeting in town,' Sue's voice was as cool as she looked.

Invited you to my house? Shingi couldn't believe what he was hearing, worse what he was seeing. He was sure that he had seen and talked to this girl before. He had been a little blazed by booze and marijuana then to notice her clearly and he was forever regretting it. And, off all the people, Anesu who had never enjoyed the pleasures of having, touching or whatever a girl was having all this goddess to himself. He grunted subconsciously. *What would Anesu do with her anyway?*

His friend was a shy person when you stripped him off all that fake charm like exterior, he thought. Shingi's sensual desires grew each second he kept his eyes on Sue.

'Yes, it's just around where we first saw each other, Anesu. Do you still remember?' Sue's eyes darted suspiciously from Anesu to Shingi.

She didn't like the look of lust that filled Shingi's eager eyes. She guessed that he was thinking of the many things he would like to do to her. She had been around men who had given her that same look and she had enjoyed it then. Now, she couldn't figure out why she felt like her body was being scanned by an unclean scanner.

Anesu saw the sudden change of her expression and sensed danger. Shingi had developed a habit of exploiting every beautiful girl he had ever got his hands on. Anesu knew his friend too well to guess that Shingi was shaken by a bout of jealousy. He couldn't blame Shingi for Sue was indeed the *brewer* of unrest. Her appearance was just too much for a man to handle. What stunned Anesu was her style of dressing. He had expected to see her in uniform that day, and hadn't imagined her as one of those young ladies who wore nothing other than tight faded jeans or clothes to show off their curvilinear structures. And a dress would have meant something much shorter, but WOW! He cursed himself for having miss-analysed her too soon.

Never judge a lady by her looks, he thought. But then, what was that she had said about inviting him to her house? That was something peculiar. Decent ladies never really invited strangers to their houses, especially strangers of the opposite sex.

Sue set forth that, instead of roaming the CBD or such, they accompany her home and promised to treat them as far as food was concerned. They agreed and walked towards the kombis.

Shingi didn't know what prompted him to do it, but the combination of wanting something to drink and smoke to cool his nerves and the desire of getting a feel of that nice body defeated his defences. He felt the arc as his hand forced its way down Sue's broad back. His nerves were re-stimulated to the extent where he did it more hungrily, pressing his hand tighter, his senses aflame with indefinable bliss. The next thing he remembered was a slap drawn so hard that it stung his senses back to the present setting.

'How dare you touch me?' Sue shrieked in a voice strangely unlike her own. Her face emphasized the shock and hatred she was heated up with. She glared murder at Shingi, who grimaced in a state of guilt. A small crowd was now audience to the scene.

Anesu was extremely furious. He had never hit anyone before, less, caught in a fist fight, but the anger he felt then made him want to strike Shingi down to eat dirt. Shingi was sparing no pains to integrate himself or even apologize. He just glared back at Sue in a painful emotion of envy.

'Anesu?'

Anesu answered the call by looking towards it. He was irritated in a dozen ways. If he was to freeze the commotion for a while, he would have personally acknowledged that, compared to what he was witnessing, Sue looked like the impression before the real deal. In a fitting faded black and white jean skirt with black flip-flops, simple long sleeved white shirt, Rebecca looked like a cutting from a beauty magazine. Her face was however lamented with disbelief.

Shingi looked at Rebecca and almost exploded with jealousy. *How could one man know so many pretty ladies like this at one time? Your mother must really be a witch.*

'My mother *a what*, Shingi? Please repeat that!'

Shingi jumped, upset by shock. *Had he thought that out loud? What the hell was happening to him?* If someone had called his mother a witch or anything profane, he knew exactly what he would have done to that person. So did Sue, Rebecca and many others who were anxiously and eagerly looking on. A physical brawl was considered inevitable, yet none occurred.

Sue looked at Anesu bewildered. He looked so dangerously calm for someone who had had his mother verbally insulted in the presence of more than ten people.

How can someone like this be friends with someone so wretched? She thought confused.

Shingi sized Anesu up and concluded that he wasn't going to take any action against him. But then, how could he? Although Anesu was tall, he himself was twice as strong and would have easily beaten him in a physical one. However, that gave him no right to insult him, but his pride prevented him from fairly expressing regret. He let the wind take its course as he glared back at Anesu challengingly.

Anesu only shook his head and looked away. Rebecca went over and held his hand whilst taking him away from the crowd towards the bus terminus. She couldn't help feeling so proud of her new friend.

'Yeah, run away, Dongo, run away with your bitches!' Shingi shouted bitterly after him.

He found himself floored and, with stars and pain, looked up to see Sue shaking her hand gasping in pain. He was up on his feet in a flash. There was no way he was going to let himself get slapped and punched by a girl and do nothing about it.

Sue stood her ground and – very scared inside, but not showing it – bravely waited for his response.

'I wouldn't dare think of it, sonny,' a tough looking man who was audience warned him against retaliating. 'As it is, you were fondling the young lady without her approval, something close to sexual abuse in the public. You deserved much more than that. If you aren't satisfied, my boys and I will deal with you personally and give you what you truly deserve, *shasha*.'

Shingi glared back at him and saw the signs of agreement from a few others behind the man. He spit the blood that had been caused by Sue's punch in front of her and slowly walked away. The crowd slowly dispersed after his departure.

'You didn't have to do that, Sue,' Anesu said softly holding her aching hand.

Sue smiled at him, suppressing the pangs of pain to do so. Her hand was slowly swelling and the pain agonizing. She looked at Rebecca and suddenly felt apprehensive. She didn't like to see someone who could be labelled as a possible threat to her beauty and this lady really made her feel small. The two ladies stared at each other, fighting a sound mental battle.

'Oh, Rebecca, this is Suri Hamilton. Suri, this is Rebecca Dongo – sorry, I mean Rebecca Rocha,' Anesu giggled and took Rebecca's hand and forced the two girls to shake hands.

Sue didn't know what infuriated her the most. Anesu titling Rebecca with his surname and trying to sound as if it hadn't been intentional or the fact that they were shaking hands together whilst a cold war had already started from the first time they had laid eyes on each other. Jealous minds led to jealous emotions, and who could fight jealousy without showing off their true emotions?

Steven knocked softly on the door and it squeaked open by the force. Somehow, it had been opened. He anxiously knocked again. He was feeling a bit disabled when an answer failed to come. He wondered if she was even at home.

'Hello, is anybody at home? *Pane vanhu here pano*?' He added in a funny Shona accent.

Subconsciously minded, he slowly let himself in. He entered directly into what looked like a sitting room. It was a little dark for the curtains weren't fully drawn. The TV was fixed at a corner, showing off pictures of a news channel. The room smelt of burnt coffee and dishwashing soap.

Steve scanned the place and at a far corner, saw a young Rebecca sandwiched between two grownups, a lady and gentleman. The photo was probably taken when she was ten or eleven years old, he thought. There was so much innocence in those childish eyes and so much intrigue as well. However, he had to admit that she had grown into a beautiful young lady. Something about her eyes made him stand and stare for a few seconds. It was like déjà vu, and yet again, he had no idea where the feeling was coming from. Maybe it was the fact that the lady in the photo had almost the same, but grown up version of Rebecca's young eyes.

A soft grunt made his attention jerk in the direction of where the kitchen was and what he saw made his heart contract. He ran over, and without thinking twice, carried the limp-like old man — rushed out of the house in a state of major unrest.

'I just don't know what to say. I'm truly sorry about Shingi. I don't know what has gotten into him nowadays. Things at home must be pretty bad for him,' Anesu stared at Sue, genuinely sad. He deeply knew that it was a lame excuse. Nothing could possibly be wrong at Shingi's home without him knowing.

Sue stared at him, her hand still hurting, but now with the familiar surroundings, she felt a bit better. She had a freezit over it, acting like an icepack. The ugly ordeal with Shingi had made them accompany Rebecca to her bus terminus in strings of restlessness. Anesu had accompanied Sue back home and had practically refused her offer to take a breather at her house. She had been hoping to prepare him some snacks, but ended up disappointed. However, it was a blessing in disguise for her hand really hurt big time.

'Please don't apologize for your friend. He went a lot overboard and if anyone should do the apologizing, it should be him. I have never met such a self-absorbed human being in my life,' Sue said waspishly, feeling her anger resurfacing. She calmed herself dearly.

'I feel sorry for him, I do. I know he didn't mean all those things he said.'

'Anesu, do you really believe that? Now you are really making me want to smack you. And what about what he did to me?'

Anesu looked down in paleness. 'I just don't know what got into him, but I believe he feels just as bad. He didn't mean it, he just lost his nerve,' he said in denial.

Dear God, are you for real? Sue wanted to shout out. *How could someone stand up for that toffee nosed fornicator after all he had done and said?* She took a long look at Anesu and felt her emotions shrink.

The guy really believed what he was saying. *He must have too much forgiveness to forgive or trust, all misguided.*

Sue wondered what she exactly saw in this guy. He was truly charming and sweet and if she were to be honest, he was a good-looking dude. It was inevitable that girls like Rebecca and her should seek his company. In the end, she knew that above all, it mostly was to do with his humble and kind nature. These were his most attractive qualities, qualities most females were a sucker for.

Overcame by oceans of emotion, Sue swung her arms around his neck and kissed him with a furious hunger and sensation of one who couldn't hold back to think about future consequences any longer. Her heart ruled her mind. Stunned, Anesu didn't respond equally at first. He didn't have any experience on such gestures of life, but he put in a performance. It was the first time he had ever kissed anyone. He felt darts of excitement spark his neurons as Sue expertly rolled her tongue around his, creating a thrilling combination of bliss and euphoria. The thrill of his soft touch as Anesu held her shoulders, the elation which possessed her, made Sue moan with pleasure.

Finally, Anesu pulled away, trying so hard to breathe. He felt weak on his toes as the residues of excitement faded slowly from his body. His strength of will completely deserted him, all his reserve sapped. He looked down at Sue and almost cried at observing her so angelic expression. She sort of squint her eyes, biting down her upper lip, observing him to witness the effects he had come out with from the passionate exchange. She tried hard not to giggle. She was experienced enough to know that Anesu had never exchanged tongues with a girl before. Sue couldn't sustain the joy of possibly having become the first girl ever to do so with him.

'What?' Anesu grinned at her. He knew now what falling in love felt like. It blocked all reason and put one in a state of total confusion. He was so confused now that he couldn't think, or was too scared to do so.

'Nothing,' Sue giggled happily. She twisted the freezit in her hands appearing like a shy individual being asked on a date and not knowing how to respond.

The silver Mercedes blocked her house's small gate and Rebecca knew it well enough to recognize it though it was getting dark at six in the evening. After all, the first time she had seen it had been nighttime.

As she entered the house, she could feel its lack of asserted activity. In cool confidence, she set her shopping bags on the table and in a decisive manner went for the kitchen.

'Grandpa, I am home,' she cried out, still dusked by the obvious reason of the Mercedes' presence.

Her grandfather's voice didn't normally come as anticipated. She called out again to be met by the echoes of her own voice. Perhaps he was asleep, or wasn't feeling too well to roam around the house. His health had been showing signs of improvement over the past few days, but he still needed his rest. She heard the front door open and close and gracefully went over to see who it was.

'What the hell are you doing here?' she shouted with an unreserved accent.

Steve, successfully dispelled, didn't answer. He just looked at her, his face darkened by an unremitting sadness. He didn't have the strength to respond.

'Mr Pye, what are you doing here?' Rebecca was more insistent and animated. Just because the man was her boss, that didn't give him the right to come to her house uninvited and unannounced.

'I'm sorry, Ms Rocha, I did all I could…' he couldn't finish for tears started crawling from his eyes.

This display made alarmed Rebecca. 'What are you talking about?' she demanded relatively mild.

Steve walked over and embraced her. Stunned, Rebecca shook and pushed him away.

'Get your hands off me, Steven!' she shouted.

If Steve could have looked disappointed, it could have been more digestible. Instead, he dropped himself into one of the sofas and drowned his head into his hands. *Just how did one break the news?* He quizzed. Of all the things he had ever been through in his life, this was the hardest and most painful of them all.

'I came around four to see you and apo… apo… pologize…' and after a few seconds of summing up all his courage, he begged her to sit and she sat on a sofa facing him. Finally, *he told her.*

He had taken Rebecca's grandfather directly to his own special family doctor, not risking the huge busy public hospital services. The man had smiled at him and given him some sort of key that now lay in his pocket. *"Rebecca"* was all he had said to Steve before the doctor and the nurses had left Steve staring after them in the Avenues Hospital corridors.

'He passed away smiling after saying your name, the doctor said. I'm terribly sorry.'

Rebecca felt dizzy, engulfed and buried by the imperious ruthless realization that this was no dream or nightmare. Grandpa was gone, taken away in the most profuse, awful of circumstances. Such a day had been inevitable, but why now? Crying silently, she looked at Steve and felt sorry for him. He had witnessed it all, watched Grandpa suffer a sudden cardiac failure and done all he could to save him, but to no avail. She rose and went over to sit beside him and tamely held his hand. It stunned Steve how so cool, calm and collected she was after hearing such news.

'Thank you, Mr Pye, thank you so much.'

And she began to release buckets of tears. Steve Pye lowered her head onto his shoulder and started bushing her hair down softly in a comforting manner. They had met by the most bizarre of circumstances and life between the two of them never made things easier.

Six

MR ZUVA stood beside Anesu in a neatly cut black suit. They had their heads cast down as the box was lowered down the grave. The air was chilly, windy and it was hard to see if anyone was still crying now. The Reverend threw the first dirt in and Rebecca followed. Despite the occasion, she looked extremely attractive in a black lady's suit, a black hat and shades.

It was the second time she was wearing that suit, and last time it had only been a few meters away where Grandma was buried. Grandpa had his wish. He was being laid to rest beside his wife's grave courtesy of an insurance package he had purchased years ago.

Sue felt saddened by watching the dead depart. It wasn't more than a month since she had buried her father. She had opted to be there not because Anesu had informed her about Rebecca's lose, but because she felt genuinely sorry for her. She had no family anymore and Sue felt like they were more alike despite her wealth and having a stepmother. She suddenly felt Steve – who stood at her side looking handsome in his black suit – squeeze her hand passionately.

Steve had done all he could, despite Rebecca's protests, at making sure that every single detail on the agenda for Grandpa Rocha's funeral went along smoothly. It had progressed on well and he hadn't believed seeing Sue at the funeral. She looked as stunning as ever, much more than what he had witnessed her in school uniform. Sue too had been as much surprised to see him. He looked up to look at Mr Zuva and fought a grin. The old man looked so eccentric with his uncombed bushy hair. The suit made him look more like a Professor. He had insisted that he accompany Steve and be at Grandpa Rocha's funeral and here they were.

Rebecca thought she saw him looking at her so many times. She didn't know if it was her grieving mind playing tricks with her or that Mr Zuva was really trying hard not to get caught staring.

They were only twelve of them, including some of Rebecca's loyal neighbours who were eventually awed by the presence of Steven Pye at Mr Rocha's burial. There was surely going to be some hot gossip floating around after the funeral, most of them thought.

By lunch, the burial was over and people dispersed. Rebecca thanked all of them for coming and they in turn gave her their best of wishes in recovery. Steven and Mr Zuva lingered a bit, and were alone for a few minutes. They ventured deep into conversation.

'This was a great thing you did, Master Steve,' he said, having a glimpse at Rebecca having a chat with one of the church ladies.

'I know you said "no", but are you sure this is wise?' Steve said anxiously. He had a glimpse of Rebecca, sadness surfacing.

Mr Zuva nodded. 'Believe me, I don't think now is the time to tell her. Give her some time to heal.'

Ten days later, Rebecca sat in her sitting room eyeing the silver key Grandpa had given to Steve. She hadn't seen it before and tried hard to figure out where it could possibly fit. The house had been left to her in the will together with all that was in it. She had been surprised to find out that Grandpa had even had one drawn. What had dazed her most was the mysterious letter that had been left addressed to an anonymous person.

The lawyer had refused to tell her who it was and had told her that she was going to find out sooner or later after he had finished carrying out one of Mr Rocha's biggest and secret wishes. It was annoying to be kept in the dark, but she knew that there was nothing she could do about it.

Actually, a few miles away, the lawyer was fuming at the daunting task Mr Rocha had left him. He wondered why the man hadn't done *it* himself when he was still alive.

Anesu found it very lonely at the factory with Rebecca away on leave. The main reason he had taken this job had been her, but her absence didn't mean he had to absent himself. The steel industry was indeed a hard place to work at. You got tired pretty early if you did small things for the body had gotten used to being used efficiently.

Thanks to Rebecca, he was now very familiar to the CEO of

Pye Industries and most of his co-workers took that as a major benefit on his end.

Take a look at Rebecca, for example, most of them thought. She was now a personal favourite of Steven Pye and only God knew if she was ever going to return to work for a man who had emotionally been deflated by her beauty. It was clear to all, that people who were born to be lucky and possess the whole package of being attractive, intelligent and level-headed like Rebecca Rocha weren't meant to work in a factory. It was considered as a waste of God's perfect creations by many at the factory.

Since that blissful day with Sue, Anesu had tried at all costs to avoid the development of such a scenario again. He didn't trust himself to be able to suppress his physical desires if such a time came. The spark between them was just too much to keep in line. However, they communicated constantly and he hadn't come out disappointed.

Sue was such a great associative individual who made him feel appreciated and far happier than he thought he deserved. And that confused him more. He was having a hard time discovering at which side of the scale his emotions weighed more. *On Sue's or Rebecca's?*

It was no secret that, before and even after the funeral, he had developed obscured, but authentic feelings for Rebecca. She was so unlike Sue, just as Sue was so unlike her. Maybe they were just friends, or maybe more, but the intimate exchange between him and Sue couldn't be mistaken as simple friendship. It had skyrocketed from nil to all.

That first kiss had ignited a flare inside him, a flare that wouldn't die. Anesu somehow understood why Shingi had suddenly turned wild and lusty towards the opposite sex over the years. It was like a drug. When you hadn't tasted it, all was okay, but the moment you tried it, it was always going to be a liability. At least his burning desires were limited towards only two ladies, and they were just enough to keep him from venturing elsewhere.

'How are you enjoying your leave?' Anesu asked Rebecca, who was sitting outside her inherited house, basking in the sunlight.

Passing by her house every time he left work after his shift had become habit. Much to his delight and amusement, she was always there. Most ladies of her age would rather have spent their time and days in town shopping or the other as some form of therapy.

Rebecca was truly an odd female character just as he seemed odder to her.

'It's boring. I wish Steve wouldn't make such a fuss that I'm not ready to come back yet. I think he is looking for a way to make me quit my job. He truly well knows that I now got only a week left on my contract there.'

Steve had even come out clean and proposed that she leave Pye Industries and concentrate on returning to uni and her upcoming attachment. Rebecca had been adamant, but as it turned out Steve shared the common likeness of being stubborn. Every time they met, that issue was hot debate.

'Maybe he is right, you know. He must have offered you some cash to go along with the deal,' Anesu conjectured Steve's idea.

'You know yourselves, men! He said it would be like some kind of loan to soothe my guilty conscience. I refused the offer,' Rebecca ended the sentence with a murmur.

Anesu raised his head and smiled.' Independent women, what silly ideas you thrust upon yourselves. It's like the story of the ugly duckling without the ugly duckling.'

Rebecca was possessed by fits of laughter. She did truly miss Grandpa and the quiet lonely house reminded her daily of her loss. But she was used to looking forward for some minutes of laughter each day because Anesu always made sure she had those whenever he passed by. She had never known a boy so exciting and fun to be around. He was constantly calm and composed every time she saw him. It was as if nothing could ever penetrate that unbelievable balm fortress. Having witnessed the ordeal between Shingi and him had made that a logical fact. She had never loved anyone other than her grandparents, but what she now felt for Anesu – could it be called *love or like?*

'Steve invited me to the company's party,' she suddenly told him.

'Oh, that. Everyone at work has been bubbling about it. It's something of celebrating the acquisition of SteelWorks by Pye Industries. Only a few VIPs will be there, I guess you are VIP,' Anesu said, a little distant.

'I don't fancy the idea. I hate social gatherings – they make me restless. I just don't look it,' Rebecca said with a defiant chin.

'If you don't look it, I'd be damned,' Anesu opposed.

'But I can't refuse the invitation, can I? I owe Steve too much to let him down on this. People at work will really have a meal out of this.'

Anesu looked at her steadily. 'No, you can't, and you look too damn beautiful to devastate your beauty on people such as me. Go out and be appreciated.'

Rebecca was more than used to Anesu's amazing openness. He was someone who said whatever was on his mind at any time, but somehow he had never been directly emotional with her. She sensed the reserve and only then was when she could detect his inborn shyness. It was surprising that he could be shy at all for he had the qualities of an ever-bickering parrot.

Another thing that made her smile always, when it came to her mind, was the fact that he never looked her directly in the eyes for more than ten seconds. The exception was only once, and that was when he had offered his condolences. It was a mystery.

Was he afraid of seeing something in her he didn't think he would like or was he just shy? No, that wasn't close to it. Whenever she saw him talking to Sue, his eyes and Sue's were always glued to each other. The two had an unbelievable extremely comfortable way toward each other, especially with Sue who wasn't afraid of physically throwing herself at Anesu whenever she was around. It crazed Rebecca, so unendurable a putrid jealously she fought endlessly. Sue was extremely attractive, charming, and talkative and perhaps that's why Anesu was so infatuated by her instead.

'You will be there, of course?' Rebecca said chasing the thoughts away.

Anesu hesitated for a while before replying. 'I guess I will. Steve is bound to ask me one way or the other. My uncle will be there too.'

'Tell me, Anesu, why can't you look me in the eyes when you talk to me? Why me? Aren't we great buddies?' Rebecca set forth, staring reflectively at the sky. It was a question that had formulated and presented itself independently.

Anesu did look at her though, unable to absorb the question. This lady was gaining the neck of someone who just asked whatever they wanted to know. And just how far would she reach into that vault for unanswered entities?

It had become almost a routine that Steve had to make a trip for home past the CBD only to return with Sue on his passenger seat. Like most things, it had started slowly and now it was like a necessity. The more he saw her, the more radiant she looked. Not a hair out of place and ever smiling.

Grandpa Rocha's funeral had somehow brought them closer to each other. They had exchanged profiles and laughed about it. Sue had even found herself telling him about all her insecurities from the past and had come out surprised when Steve had merely laughed. Her worries were however currently centred on this new lady she had met not long ago. Rebecca was appearing to be something of an indirect threat to her mental state. It had all had to do with emotions.

How was it possible that Rebecca knew Anesu, whilst at the same time Steve knew her as well? The two men she adored the most in her reformed life had a thing for that other girl. It was so rare a coincidence.

The news that Rebecca was a medical student, a forthcoming doctor, only amplified her envy for the lady. Most annoyingly, unlike herself who had many skeletons in her closets, Rebecca seemed purely magical with none. You could find no fault in her, no flaw and she was definitely someone you would love to hate.

Choice was also another problem for Sue. Who appealed to her the most – the wealthy famous Steven Pye or the irresistible-adorable Anesu Dongo? With Rebecca in the background, it was grossly a choice even to consider making.

'Are you still up to it for tomorrow?'

Sue looked up and realized that her mind was wavering. It was a cool Friday evening and Sue was doing some shopping for both her and stepmom. She was now the proud owner of a Mazda 3, having chosen to buy the least expensive, but socially adequate car she could get. It was interesting that if she wanted, she could have even bought a Rolls Royce or Ferrari with the wealth she had, and yet she was choosing to live simple. She could have bought a huge mansion or went to live in one of her inherited properties and yet she had chosen to live in a small suburb. She wondered a lot why she was laying this low.

She was just from school, still in uniform and had unexpectedly run into Steven, his amiable father and Mr Zuva. It was the first time she saw Richard Pye in person and couldn't agree more that he was an affable and interesting man. Steve had managed to persuade Mr Zuva to accompany his father over the wine section to choose a perfect collection for the upcoming party. Mr Zuva had happily given in seeing that Steve and Sue must have needed some time alone.

'Sorry, Steve, you were saying?'

'Evidently you got your mind elsewhere, hey. I was speaking of the party tomorrow, at my house. You aren't having second thoughts, are you? The anxiety of meeting my father must have passed now thanks to coincidence,' Steve took a spray can of deodorant from her trolley and grinned at its brand.

'That's Mum's,' Sue snatched it back. 'I don't know what to say. It's true that I have been having doubts. Not because I'm scared of anything to do with meeting a few business executives from big companies. As you know, I have done it before, although in the weirdest of occasions thanks to Mum and Dad. It's only that I was supposed to be going to Watershed tomorrow with the school's volleyball team and return on Sunday and I had to make up some interesting excuse to the coach, not mentioning my teammates. But don't worry, it's a little sacrifice for you and for fun.'

'Thanks, Sue, you are a life-saver,' Steve put a passionate arm around her shoulder and squeezed it thankfully.

The nearness of their bodies made him feel excited for a while and he had to pull away when he saw Mr Zuva and his father curiously eyeing them. The grins they gave him made him shudder in embarrassment.

Sue felt as happy as if she was on cloud nine before she caught the envious glances from other women in that shop. Steve was a formidable bachelor, and being a rich and handsome one for that matter made any lady who was seen with him *gossip* women's enemy number one, especially when you were so young and attractive and wearing a school uniform for that matter. Many thought she was his mistress, being treated by the Pye's limitless golden credit card. All they could think of was that she was an upcoming gold digger, whilst some were lenient enough to designate her as possibly his cousin sister for it wasn't actually news that there was only one heir to the Pye Empire and it was a *he*.

The Roots and Stems

THE PARTY was full of odds and evens, statistically abbreviated with idioms of peace and unrest. Sue had appeared at the party wearing a long blue dress that clung to her curvy body and emphasized her beauty. She had outshone the majority of women at the gathering.

Many potential candidates to Steve's hand in marriage were openly intimidated when Steve had gently walked over to escort her in. Men alike had tried hard to keep their eyes off Sue, but in the end, it had seemed inevitable. Her charming smile and air made her look senior her age. Sue enjoyed her reign as the *Star* for about thirty minutes and when that other lady she was afraid of finally arrived, she knew it was over.

Rebecca had chosen to come in a plain high-necked knee-length black dress. Her appearance made a lot of people stare and stutter. It was so amazing how one could turn such a simple dress to appear so devastatingly appealing and seductive. It wasn't about the dress. It was about the person in the dress. Anesu stood positively beside her in a black suit and together they looked the perfect pair. Sue couldn't tear her eyes from them, partly apprehensive, partly intrigued. The two ladies greeted each other politely and went over the drinks' section to prepare something to sip.

'Nice party you are having here,' Rebecca complimented before drawing a long sip. She was feeling a bit uneasy. 'You look stunning.'

'It's an okay function, but if I look stunning then what would we call you? I simply don't know how you do it. Everything seems to fit on you without reservation,' Sue replied truthfully. They giggled girlishly.

'It was the only good dress I had that was still new-looking,' Rebecca told her smoothing the dress down.

'I can even buy the most expensive of dresses and won't be able to compete with you in simple attire. That is kinda annoying if you know what I mean,' Sue said with a grin.

Rebecca didn't know if it was an ironic or genuine remark. She liked and respected Sue, but whenever Sue saw her and Anesu together, Sue always gave her a look that made her shiver. It was more like when she herself saw Steve and Sue together.

'Sir, I don't know why you think or why you even doubt that human resource management is maidenly effective in all spectrums of modern business,' Anesu was consumed in a broad discussion with none other than Mr Zuva. 'I worked at my mother's bank last semester and I witnessed its effectiveness.'

Mr Zuva looked neat in a brownish checked suit and someone had convinced him at least to run a comb in his wild bush of white and black hair. The man looked disquietly familiar in a distant way to Anesu and he couldn't decode the meaning other than that they had first met at a funeral.

'Your mother works at a bank, you say? What does she do?'

'She is an Architect by profession, but she also holds an MBA, so at the bank she is a HR Manager,' Anesu said proudly.

'And your father?'

Anesu looked down, a sadness colouring upon him. He didn't like talking about his father. He wondered if it would seem rude if he said so. He barely knew this man, only that he was the Pye's friend and the man barely knew him.

'He left when I was young. My mother raised me as a single parent.'

'Oh, I'm sorry about that, Master Anesu, I'm sorry indeed. It is unfortunate that we now live in a world of single parenthoods,' Mr Zuva looked down almost ashamed. He didn't have such a clean past. 'So you believe in that type of management facilitation?'

'I believe it works, for the better good in organisations with an economy such as ours, sir.'

'Master Anesu, it is nothing other than manipulative. It is after all largely an empirical question, but so far little has been done to resolve it one way or the other.'

'How would you know, sir?'

'My dear young sir, it is my job to know. I'm writing a thesis on it for my doctorate in Philosophy, Master Anesu. But then, questions can't be answered in the abstract although they are nearly always posed thus,' Mr Zuva said wisely, looking down at him with a smile.

He liked this young man. Unlike Steve who had been born and bred in money, Anesu possessed the natural ability to both observe and see. That much he could derive.

'I should have guessed so. You sound like one of my professors – I can barely understand what you are saying at times.'

'And what will those people of culture be teaching you, Master Anesu?'

Anesu shrugged and returned Sue's wave from a distance. 'Architectural Science, sir.'

'Ahhh, I like it. Following in your mother's footsteps I presume.'

Anesu nodded with a grin. 'I'm sure she wouldn't have had it any other way. She tends to be rather possessive when it comes to what I do with my life. Where did you do your other degrees, sir?' he said, very curious. He was wondering a lot where Mr Zuva knew the Pyes. He was yet to discover their relationship.

'Brunel University, Master Anesu, at the broad island of Lady England. I went there during a time when going to learn abroad was rather a huge thing than it is nowadays. I spent more than fifteen years there. Unfortunately, I only reached half of my doctorate and returned to become a, live a…' Mr Zuva's eyes faded as he remembered. 'A pretty mobile life before Master Pye found me. Bless his soul.'

Steve managed to get hold of Rebecca's hand after she was exchanged from one businessman to another. She was an exciting guest who amused her pursuers in association. They all wanted to know who she was. She had to get away by telling them that she was an employee at Pye Industries, avoiding giving much detail on the matter.

Steve was so excited. He had been given approval to present his *surprise* to her that night. He hadn't even thought of how odd it was that she didn't *know* after all this time. Her presumed reaction was going to be *something*, he thought.

'I think I have met almost everyone, Steve,' Rebecca followed, laughing in his brisk footsteps. 'Why the sudden rush, hey?'

'This one is special,' Steve said mysteriously. 'I hope you'll forgive me for having kept you in the dark for so long. It wasn't my intention to do so.'

'Come on, Steve, you are now scaring me. Who is this person?'

Steve and Rebecca reached Anesu and Mr Zuva and exchanged laughs. They talked for about ten minutes before Rebecca suddenly remembered where they had been heading or had it been just Steve's trick to get her away from the other men for himself?

'Aren't we supposed to be seeing this special person of yours, Steve?' she asked merrily.

The look she gave Steve made him tremble a little with excitement.

'I don't know how to do this, but I'll just do it. Rebecca, dear, do you see anything familiar?' Steve said.

Rebecca looked around and only saw the two people that stood in front of them. She shook her head confused. 'No, what is it?'

Steve let it sink and only grinned. Rebecca smiled back. Anesu grinned in the process, witnessing the exchange of strokes between the two. He wondered why he wasn't the bit jealous.

'Let me help you on that one, Master Steve,' Mr Zuva answered for him with a weak smile. 'I returned from the UK a few years ago, after having made something of myself there. The life here had completely changed. What I heard and saw in the media abroad was a total misrepresentation of what I thought I'd find here.'

'Life has surely changed these past few years here in Zim,' Rebecca offered. She had experienced it first hand, from the change in economy, infrastructure, policies and many more.

'Why did you return, sir, I'm sure many wouldn't come back from a first world country to what we have here. The transition is almost painful, unless of course one has a lot of money.'

'Money wasn't a problem, Master Anesu. My family was privileged with quite a sum-full. What would anyone want other than money?' he said with a smile.

'Love?' Rebecca said subconsciously.

Mr Zuva looked at her and smiled with a nod. 'I returned for a *woman* I had left when I left for UK. I was determined to find her.'

'Were you in constant touch with her?' Rebecca asked. She wondered where this story was going.

'I wasn't, although technology could have made it possible. My family were too critical about her, so was her family toward me. She did come from a traditional and strict family. Communication was rather difficult especially since we both lived in Marondera.'

'But then you returned for her and, forgive my scepticism, but fifteen years is rather a long time. A lot of things could have happened then,' Anesu said analytically.

The party seemed to have faded away from the group as they listened to Mr Zuva's tale.

'That is definitely true. I didn't know anything, but curiosity had had the better of me. I did return mainly to search for business investments, keep the Zuva name existent in the country I grew up. When I returned, I searched for her, but her parents were long dead and I couldn't trace any relation. All of them had left Marondera, either for other cities or abroad. The only thing I could find out about her from one of her old neighbours was that she had been pregnant and her father hadn't been so merciful when her young daughter had carried a child out of wedlock. She had been chased away from home and the neighbour didn't know what had happened to her. It wasn't to my knowledge that I had left her marred with such a burden and I'll not excuse our immaturity then. I felt so terrible and guilty.

After a year of failing to find her or any link to her, I felt like my life was extinguished from me, for the love I had for her was like an addiction and had been what had kept me going through the years of my studies. I ignored my duties back in UK, treated myself badly, lost hope and was succumbed by the death of consciousness. I had no reason to survive for I too no longer had any family left in the country to comfort me. I was willing to adjust myself to the environment. Pain and loss of self-determinism destroyed my will to live, so I lived only to live, but not to live.'

The others stared at him with awe. It was a touching story. Anesu was however very confused. Mr Zuva didn't look like a failure. He looked the opposite.

'Just when I thought it was all over, flooded by suicidal tendencies, almost in succeeding, you redeemed me, Ms Rocha. You brought me back from my greybeard unconsciousness. I haven't done it or will ever be able to fully, but I thank you for saving my life, Ms Rocha, it cannot be enough.'

Rebecca was clouded by confusion. 'I'm sorry, I what? I don't understand what you are saying, sir.'

But it later dawned on her when she looked closer and distinguished Mr Zuva's mouth. It was a mouth she could barely forget for it was somehow printed in her sense data. Her breath quickened as she was filled with both emotion and confusion. She let out a soft scream.

'You are the *tramp*? I... I... I...' she paused to catch her breath, hastily staring from Steve to Mr Zuva. 'I applied CPR on you? It's you. Wow! I can't believe it – I can't... Wow!'

'Please do, Ms Rocha. I recovered well and Master Pye and his father were blessed to take me under their care. I owe you and them my life. Bless you all eternally.'

Rebecca threw numerous questions at Steve and Mr Zuva and in about ten minutes, all of them were oblivious of the party and the guests around them.

'This is truly remarkable,' Rebecca said happily, glowing with happiness. Steve beamed at her expressions. The secret had been worth keeping. He was enjoying each second of the revelation. 'Like a fairy tale.'

'It could have been if I found Thelma and what happened to her and our child,' Mr Zuva said.

'I'm sorry, but what did you say?' Anesu's expression suddenly turned pale.

'I said it could have been a fairy tale if I found the woman I was telling you about, Thelma.'

To Rebecca it was like a fairy tale with an unusual happy ending. To Mr Zuva it was glamour and glory of the joy to tell her everything at last. To Steve, it was the enjoyment of watching Rebecca's beautiful face in diverse expressions. But to Anesu, it was something of a vision, an untouchable shocker by which he wasn't positive he would recover.

'Anesu, are you alright?' Rebecca asked him concerned. He looked like he was fighting a bout of flu and nausea.

'Mr Zuva, er...,' he stuttered. 'I'm sorry to ask, but what is Thelma's full name?'

'Why, yes, Master Anesu. I can never forget it. It's permanent read only memory,' Mr Zuva said, surprised by the sudden question. 'It's Thelma Dongo, daughter of Mr Henry Dongo, a very stern and feisty man during his time. You have no idea how many Dongos they are in the country – my search was vast. If she got married, it must have somehow changed as such long back.'

'Oh my God,' Anesu was in tears and it was the most embarrassing yet odd situation for the others to witness.

Now what was that all about?

Only Rebecca looked shocked at the possibilities, staring hard at Anesu as if trying to read his mind.

'Master Anesu, please compose yourself. What is wrong?' Mr Zuva's said.

'My mother is called Thelma Dongo. Henry junior is my uncle's middle name,' Anesu offered like a calm whisper.

Mr Zuva staggered back. He looked like a shark and a dolphin at the same time, eyes unblinking treasured by a shock so severe.

'Good Lord, dear Lord,' Anesu shook his head and walked away tears dripping at whim.

Rebecca followed him at a distance enough to give him his personal space and endure. Some guests stared after them stunned. Rebecca caught hold of Anesu just as he was about to exit. She inserted her hand through his elbow, followed. Anesu was too distraught to react.

On the outside, the evening was a bit chilly, the stars shinning up there. Half of the moon made light. Anesu plugged his hands into his pockets, looked out into the atmosphere. Rebecca released his hand, looked at him, waiting.

'Is it what I think it is, Anesu?' she finally said.

Anesu looked at her, was touched by her caring expression. He said nothing, tried to smile. He produced a weak smile in the end.

'It is, isn't it?' Rebecca persisted.

'I just found out, at a party I could have never attended if I had never met you, that, that...' he couldn't finish.

Rebecca stepped in closer. Two guests exited, nodded politely at them, went in the direction of where the cars were parked. Rebecca and Anesu watched them go. Rebecca's gaze returned on him.

'That the man I saved, of all the people in the world, could possibly, is highly likely, your father?' she said softly, shocked. She looked at him searching for *something*. She saw something she had never seen in him and it scared her. For once, Anesu looked weak and vulnerable. 'How can it be true?'

'I'd like to believe that it's not, but my mother...' he paused, winced as if in pain. 'My mother is Thelma, and the story fits the few pieces my uncle told me when I once asked him about my origin.'

The two stood there, uncertain of what the future held. Suddenly, they looked back to see someone exit the house. It was Mr Zuva. Behind him was Steve. They all stared at each other, the environment so awkward for all. Anesu looked away into the night. Rebecca stared at him, moved in closer and put a comforting hand on his shoulder. She turned, smiled politely at Mr Zuva and left with Steve.

'Now that was something else,' Steve said as the two headed back to the party. 'I can't imagine anything beating that.'

'Tell me about it,' Rebecca said still shocked. 'It's so unbelievable.'

'I want you to meet someone,' Steve said.

Rebecca looked up at him and saw him blushing. She got a bit sceptic. Those words had been said not long ago and they had produced things she couldn't have dreamed of ever. 'Who?'

'Your boss,' Steve said.

He led her through the crowd to an area that was mostly composed with elder men playing poker. The men looked nothing, but wealth and retired. The area felt superior, unique.

Richard Pye looked up to see his son and smiled proudly. His gaze then strayed at Steve's side and rested on Rebecca. All of a sudden, his expression changed. He went pale. Rebecca saw this and was a bit taken aback by the hostile expression. *Did she look that bad for the famous Richard Pye?*

'Dad,' Steve said. He gestured aside.

The men sitting with his father raised their wine glasses to him, and he saluted back. Richard left his colleagues, went to where the two were.

'This is Rebecca, Dad,' Steve introduced her.

Richard eyed her hard and long, took her hand and produced a smile. 'How are you young lady, I am Richard Pye.'

Rebecca giggled. 'It's an honour to meet you, sir. Your son has told me quite a lot about you.'

'All good things, I hope.'

There was brief laughter. Richard had her eyes on her – they didn't waver. Rebecca kind of felt uneasy at his steady gaze. *What was wrong?*

'Young Steve, please come here boy. Let's have a talk whilst you stand in for your father. Perhaps I can win some of my money back,' one of the men from the poker table shouted at him.

Steve looked at Rebecca, undecided. Rebecca nodded, smiled at him. He grinned back and left her with Richard. Rebecca looked back at Richard and found him still staring. She smiled back politely.

Richard finally shook his head clear. 'I'm sorry to stare, but can you please come with me, young lady, just for a while. I want to introduce you to my lady of the house,' he prompted.

Rebecca was surprised. *Why would Steve's father want to introduce her to the lady of the house, whoever she was? Did Richard Pye think that Steve wanted to marry her and show her off?*

At that time, Ms Sandati was in the kitchen, directing the cleaning of the huge mounds of dirty dishes from the party to a few handy aids. Richard walked in with Rebecca, nodded to the greetings he received from the aids. Ms Sandati looked up, was very surprised to see him.

The party was surely not over yet for Mr Pye to visit the kitchen for any reason whatsoever. Her eyes fell on Rebecca. She stared hard at her.

'Mr Pye, what are you doing here?' she asked.

'Sorry to budge in on you, I want you to meet Steve's friend,' Richard said.

Rebecca walked over, her hand raised, a polite smile. Something about this lady was magnetic to her. She looked friendly, quite pretty and her eyes, there was something about her eyes.

Ms Sandati could believe she was Steve's friend. She was gorgeous in all means. *Was this the girl Richard had been telling her about? Wasn't her name called Sue-something?* 'I am Ms Sandati.'

'My name is Rebecca.'

'Rebecca?' Ms Sandati was surprised.

'Yes, that's me. Steve's friend as Mr Pye here kindly pointed out.'

Ms Sandati stared at her, for too long for Rebecca's liking.

What was it with these people and staring? Did they have to scrutinize her that much since she was Steve's friend? Did all of Steve's female friends go through this process?

'Rebecca, tell me, what's your second name or are you already Steve's prospect?' Ms Sandati said in a lovely friendly voice, heading for the cabinets.

The others had laughed.

'It's Rocha, Ms Sandati,' Rebecca replied.

The dishes Ms Sandati was transporting to the cabinets all fell, smashed and disintegrated on the marble floor of the kitchen. Richard seeing this only managed to turn blue, clutch his chest and collapsed.

The Avenues Hospital was filled with influential people. Richard

Pye had had a heart attack. And it had been *her* fault, Rebecca had claimed blaming herself.

'You know, I feel like I am in a dream, Steve. A wild, wild, wild dream. First Anesu, then this,' Rebecca sat sadly on the chair that made her look at Richard's hospital bed. 'How can Ms Sandati be my mother and your father be my father?'

Steve shook his head, his face lamented with nothing, but uncertainty. 'I'm totally in loss of words or even what to think.'

Rebecca looked back at him. She felt faint. 'I can't think clearly too. What did Ms Sandati say?'

'It was hard to get her out of her room to talk to me. She couldn't stop crying. I managed to get little out of her and she told me that your grandpa's lawyer saw her yesterday and it all fits. She changed her name to obtain South African citizenship after leaving you in the hands of your grandmother. And it turns out that Sandati was your grandmother's maiden name.'

'But I was registered as a Rocha?' Rebecca said, staring at Richard who lay peacefully in bed.

'That was your grandpa's doing, after Ms Sandati failed to tell him who your real father was. It also seems like Dad was in love, or has always been in love with Ms Sandati. I think that's the main reason she migrated back from SA when my mother died. Your mother had been commuting up and down from there until she finally thought of coming back to cater for you, but couldn't find your grandparents or something. She has spent all these years searching with no success, she said. There are a lot of secrets there, things that don't make sense.'

'This means that we are related,' Rebecca stared down.

Steve grinned, staring outside the windows. 'Indeed we are, dear sister, indeed we are.'

Rebecca closed her eyes and found herself querying and healing all the questions that came to her. She was biologically a Pye – Steven's half-sister. It was something she had never dreamt of, but fate had its own definition. What was it that made one less aware of the brilliance of the world around them? The world hadn't changed, but the roses in it had.

...the start